This book belongs to

. . . .

Greenville

Greenville
Where Longing Meets Loss

Mary Warner

This book is a work of fiction. The characters and events within are purely the products of the author's imagination and should not be construed as real. Any resemblence to actual events or people, living or dead, is entirely coincidental.

Published by Woo Woo Teacup Publishing, Little Falls, MN
http://www.woowooteacup.com
http://woowooteacup.wordpress.com

Keeping Edition: ISBN-13: 978-0-9822241-0-6
                 ISBN-10: 0-9822241-0-9

Book design & layout: Mary Warner
Author photo: Copyright © 2007 by Erik Warner
Other cover photos: Copyright © 2008 by Mary Warner

For my family &
for town characters everywhere

———————

In memory of LeRoi Moore
(1961-2008)

Acknowledgements

This is the most difficult section of a book to write for me, not because I'm miserly and ungrateful, but because my gratitude stretches beyond words. Therefore, I shall pretend this is the Grammy Awards and I have only so much time before the orchestra starts playing to list everyone who supported the writing of this book.

Dave Matthews Band (DMB) - for the original inspiration for Stories 1 and 2

Marty Nolan of Red Light Management - for handling my permissions request related to DMB's music and this book and for gamely responding to other music-related emails I sent

Andy Weissberg of R. R. Bowker - for answering my questions about ISBNs

Gwen at Shelley Funeral Chapel, Dorothy at Morrison County Veterans Services, and Dave at the Minnesota State Veterans Cemetery - for helping me figure out why a veteran's hat is sometimes placed in his/her hands during a funeral

Aubrey Immelman - for reading "Miss Fortune" with an eye toward my accuracy in regards to South Africa and the Boer War (any remaining inaccuracies are purely my fault)

My blog readers - for encouraging me by asking when this book would be finished and available for purchase

The Great River Writers - for listening to portions of my work in progress and for giving me suggestions for naming my blog, which led to it being called The Woo Woo Teacup Journal

Eric Swanson - for hosting my website and for answering sticky technology-related questions

Ann Marie Johnson, Cindy Moore, and Jody Scott-Olson - all great friends and fabulous writers in their own right who read through drafts and gave me invaluable advice about what worked and what didn't

The Morrison County Historical Society - for giving me an intricate knowledge of the history of small town life and the inner workings of a museum by employing me

Teddy Matteson - the town character who used to watch over my desk at work

And, finally . . .

My lovin' spouseful Erik and the three sweetest offspring in the whole world, Eldest Son, Daughter, and Young Son Number Two - for giving me time to write, for listening to me talk about Greenville, and for encouraging me to be just who I am.

A hearty thank you and hugs to everyone for your assistance and support.

I think the orchestra's playing now.

Contents

Longing

A knot of breathlessness perched atop her diaphragm, leaving her expectant, fearful. She was in a strange position, lying face down with her left arm crooked over her head, her fingers twined through and pulling her hair. She felt the knot against the mattress, like the princess's pea from the fairytale that her mother used to read to her. As she rolled over and opened her eyes, sunlight erased fragments of fitful dreams. The knot wanted to work its way to her throat, where she was sure it would release and bring relief, but it was trapped and her chest ached with its mass.

Lenore sat up and propped her pillows against the headboard. She leaned back to lengthen her stomach and slowly inhaled. On the out breath she hissed through her teeth. The knot remained. "What is wrong with me?" she said aloud to her bedroom walls. She felt silly, like a whisper was wiser, even though the house was hers alone.

Maybe if I get moving, go do something, I can shake this, she thought. She rose, decided to skip a shower, but washed her face, armpits and hands, applied extra deodorant and deftly inserted contacts. She pulled a soft gray track suit from her dresser drawer. The color matched her mood, although the white stripes along the sides were pushing the edge of cheerfulness. While dressing, Lenore opted for a gray tank top instead of a bra. The bra would just constrict the knot in her chest. Even though she would be out in public, she had no fear of men ogling her breasts. She had a shapely figure, average pretty face, and medium-length, dark coppery hair, but Lenore knew that her personality didn't bubble in a way that caused people, especially men, to notice her.

Over a breakfast of orange juice and corn flakes, Lenore scanned the morning paper. Perhaps there was something interesting going on in Greenville today that could lift her out of her funk. She was not likely to participate, however. During her Wednesdays off, she followed a routine that varied little from week to week. If she had errands, she ran them in the morning. Without a car, this could take some time because she either walked or had to wait for the bus. She preferred to walk, but this generally caused her obligations to stretch into the afternoon. A bag lunch of peanut butter and jelly sandwich, fruit, sweet snack, and bottled water went with her for this eventuality. When she completed her "must do" list, Lenore spent the rest of the day wandering about town.

Today was a good Wednesday, or should have been had she not had a sticky knot to untangle. There were no errands; the day was free, which meant she could visit the monkeys at the Greenville Zoo. They never failed to raise her spirits.

Lenore finished her breakfast, pulled on tennis shoes, stuffed her lunch and water into a tote, safety-pinned a house key to her waistband, and stepped out her front door. She drew in another long breath on the stoop and sniffed the earthy spring air. It was simply delicious. She imagined that munching on wet dirt was one benefit of being a worm. With no tongue, a worm didn't have to deal with the gritty texture that repulsed human beings.

Lenore's house looked out on Gray Street. She sighed. *How dismal. Why couldn't my parents have picked Orange or Indigo or even Ochre Street for our home?*

Early in the history of Greenville, the town fathers thought it would be a good idea to play off the city's color name and continued the theme for street names. The streets ran east and west out from the town's central feature, the

Mud River, which ran like an alimentary canal feeding Greenville's economy. Street names crossed the river in an effort by city surveyors to unify the two sides of town. The oldest streets carried primary and secondary color names, such as Red, Blue, Purple, Green and Yellow. North/south avenues were conventionally numbered: First, Second, Third, Fourth. As Greenville expanded, it moved south-ward. A band of neutrally named streets, including Brown, Tan, Gray, and Black, cropped up alongside the original section of town.

From Black Street, White was an obvious next choice. Unfortunately, someone got a little too enamored with the whites and this area of town became thoroughly confus-ing with its White, Ecru, Off-white, Eggshell, and Titanium White Streets. All the whites blended together making it impossible to remember their order by visualizing them. And wouldn't you know it? Those who lived on the white-based streets kept their neighborhoods as stark and clean as an interior designer's minimalist fantasy. It dawned on Lenore that her mother had been fussy enough to live in that part of town, bauble-collector though she was. Her mother had owned hundreds of knick-knacks, but she kept each one dust-free and perfectly placed, just as the grass in the white section of town was kept weed-free and well coifed. Gray Street must have been her father's choice.

As the city radiated outward and sprouted suburbs, color names became a virtual paint chip array. There was Misty Mauve Street, Lemon Delight Boulevard, and Butter-nut Beige Circle. Lenore changed her mind. Gray Street was definitely better than some of the alternatives. She bounced down the stoop, temporarily buoyed by the fresh air and low, gauze-covered, early sunshine, and checked her mail-box. The mail carrier didn't come by until around three, but that didn't stop her from looking anyway. Upon finding the box empty, the knot rumbled and the sense of expectancy rose, along with anxiety. She felt as though she was missing something, but she knew not what. Motion would help, if not to remove the feeling, at least to deaden it, so she turned east and walked down Gray Street.

Seventeen blocks separated Lenore's home from the zoo. The path she took was a familiar one as she walked to work almost every day and her place of employment was located just a block from the zoo. Down Gray Street for eight blocks, then south on Eighth Avenue past Black Street, through the Whites, over Ochre Street, where she worked as a truck dispatcher, and finally to Burnt Sienna; her mind remained blessedly empty as her legs delivered her to the main gate of the Greenville Zoo. Two dead oak trunks, seven-feet tall and chain-sawed into the likeness of bears, stood sentinel and greeted her as she entered. They looked a little grumpy today.

Lenore paid the entry fee. The zoo wasn't busy on Wednesday mornings, so she didn't have to wade through crowds to get to her favorite exhibit, the snow monkeys. She tried to arrive by feeding time because the monkeys were most active then. Billie, the dominant male, was forever chasing the younger, meeker monkeys away from his fresh fruit and greens, thumping them a good one if they managed to get close enough. Sometimes he made the mistake of throwing food at the other monkeys in order to drive them away. When they snatched it and ran, he screamed. The dominant female, Trish, hovered and cooed around Billie. During his rages, she sneaked up to him in a cower and brushed and picked his fur in order to calm him. She often dodged Billie's flailing arms. After bickering over food and exchanging a bout of swinging, proud stances and hoots, the full-stomached monkeys settled into a doze.

Lenore wondered at the monkey behavior, especially the solicitude of Trish toward Billie. The constant groveling must get old, even for monkeys. Lenore's mother had never kowtowed to her father. The guys Lenore worked with would say that her father was whipped, but that wasn't it. He had adored her mother and felt that giving her the world was his privilege. Lenore knew that many relationships never played out as well as the one her parents had had. Those that mimicked the monkeys were all too common – horrifying dramas that were sometimes fun to watch, but no fun to live through. Normally, Lenore allowed the drama to cheer her, avoiding all comparisons of monkey relationships to human ones. Today was not one of those days. She attributed the dark thoughts to the knot in her stomach, which was playing with her breakfast and producing heartburn.

It was time to move again. As she left the zoo, she threw some change into the violin case of a man who could only properly be described as a town character. Known as the Tin Man, he seemed ageless yet ancient and was familiar to young and old. His appearance never altered. He wore the same rumpled, but spotless, chocolate brown suit every day. Lenore thought this a sensible way to dress as it eliminated all the wasted minutes used in fussing over what to wear. The Tin Man accessorized his outfit with one black dress shoe and one brown, and a wind-up gold pocket watch with which he would share the time if asked. When it was chilly, he donned a brown, stuffed parka. He spent his mornings outside the zoo gate collecting donations in his frayed violin case with no violin apparent. In the afternoons, the Tin Man might show up anywhere around town with the same case and mission. As he stood over his violin case, he swayed and hummed and, without making eye contact, nodded toward whoever chucked coins his way.

Although his behavior and dress indicated otherwise, Lenore knew the Tin Man was not homeless. He lived down on the Mud River Flats in a little house - most would call it a shack - covered with bits of tin and aluminum, mostly in the form of pop cans, hence his nickname. His family and his house had played a central role in the founding history of the town, although few people remembered that now. Lenore's parents told her about the Tin Man when she had first spotted him at the zoo as a child.

Leroy Jarbeau was his given name. As a young man, he fell desperately in love with a fashionable young lady named

Pomeline Foil. She granted him her hand in marriage but he was drafted into World War II before they wed. By the time he returned, she had run off with some greasy weasel of a guy who had promised her chocolate-and-roses romance and picket-fence security. Besides, he made Pomeline feel gorgeous in a way that Leroy never got around to. According to rumor, the guy told Pomeline to keep Leroy's engagement ring because her beau would probably be killed in the war and there was no sense in throwing away a perfectly good diamond. He promptly married her before they left town, with Leroy's ring serving as Pomeline's wedding ring. The rat didn't even bother to buy his own wedding band. Pomeline died by her own hand in 1946, after a couple of years of wretched treatment from her husband. Leroy was heartbroken, more over Pomeline's suicide than of her abandonment of him. His thinking was that if she was alive, perhaps one day she could be his again. With death, that was impossible. At Pomeline's funeral, her parents had given the ring back to Leroy and he supposedly still wore it on a chain around his neck hidden beneath his brown suit.

It was the saddest story Lenore had ever heard when she was growing up. Recalling it now caused the knot in her chest to swell. Her breath came in gasps as she walked west along Burnt Sienna Street toward the Mud River. Poor Leroy Jarbeau had lost all hope, his days and years an endless, lonely roving. *How can he bear to live?* thought Lenore. She stopped to suck in air. Tears pushed at the corners of her eyes. She pressed them back, making her fingers ward off the threat of them spilling onto her cheeks. *God! How stupid!* Here she was, almost crying over a man she did not know. "Enough already!" she said. Her self-inflicted scolding did the trick. The knot settled back into place. The tears did not come.

Lenore continued her circuitous path. She traversed First Avenue and approached the Mud River Road, the one street between her and the river. The Mud River Road had become a designated scenic byway a few years back because there was very little development between it and the river. The handful of mills that leeched water power from the river during Greenville's industrial era had long since been removed. There were two reasons the prime river property remained undeveloped. First, the road, originally an old Indian trail, ran so close to the river in town that building on the flats was impractical. Flooding was assured in high-water years. Secondly, the forward-thinking city council was interested in keeping the river corridor wild for tourism purposes. The river banks throughout town served as an almost continuous public access park.

When Lenore reached the Mud River Road, she crossed and entered the park. Wood chip walkways softened her steps as she headed toward the river bank, angling slightly north. She searched out her favorite seat, a living willow downed in a wind storm, but root-bound enough to val-iantly cling to the soil and continue growing. Its trunk ran parallel to and out over the water, creating a bench for park visitors. Lenore took off her tennis shoes, cramming her socks into the toes. She pulled her lunch sack and water bottle out of the tote, then left the tote with her shoes at the base of another nearby willow.

A grumble in Lenore's stomach joined the knot as she climbed onto the tree to eat her lunch. "Just what I need – a blood sugar drop to make me even crankier than I already am." She wasn't sure if she had said this last thought aloud, but it didn't matter. The park seemed deserted and the surrounding willow branches wept a protective veil that kept anyone from peering at her as she ate. This spot on the bank, an alcove really, was an especially good one for skinny dipping, or so she had heard. No one had ever taken her for a naked midnight swim.

She finished her lunch and wistfully swung her feet in the water, splashing and splashing droplets at the min-nows. The little fish had the biggest eyes, eyes that bulged and floated on the surface of their silver faces. When she was small, she liked to try to catch minnows, but they were too quick and the light refraction put them out of reach of her aim. Her father knew the secret to nabbing the flashing skinny-bullet bodies and he would hold one in his hand so she could gently poke it with a forefinger. The fish's gills had madly searched for oxygenated water as it lay on its side. Its eye looked desperate and distant. She begged her father to let it go. It belonged in the river and she was glad that she had never learned how to grab the fish or its relatives. All the same, she liked to share the water with them and she did so now, hopping off the willow trunk and allowing mud to ooze through her toes.

The water was spring-time cold. Even though the sun was high and bright, it would not warm the river until mid-summer. Lenore suddenly had to pee. She gathered her tote and tennis shoes and sprinted through the park. Luckily, Lenore's yard on Gray Street abutted the Mud River Road so she didn't have far to go. She unlocked the door and bolted through it, tossing her things to the floor.

Her bladder relieved, Lenore entered the living room and plopped onto an over-stuffed floral couch. She could never bring herself to claim the thing. It was a tad sweet and overdone for her taste, but was the perfect expression of her mother. Through the misfortune of her parents' deaths, Lenore had inherited the house along with its attendant furniture and this God-awful couch. For years now, she had been unable to muster the energy to redecorate, though she kept telling herself, "One of these days . . . ." Instead, she covered the offensive print with a comforter and tried to ignore her tendency toward laziness.

She aimed the remote at the television and clicked through several channels. She paused on a national news network, caught by the story of a sixteen-year-old Greenville boy who could heal people by speaking in tongues at them. The boy had disappeared, but no one could determine whether he had gone into hiding of his own volition or had been forced out of the spotlight by his handlers. Lenore wished that he could perform his woo-woo magic on her.

Maybe then she could figure out what was bothering her.

A moment later, her knot lurched. She tasted sour bile and swallowed hard to keep from gagging. The newscaster had reported a story about a threatened nation-wide trucker strike. As far as she was concerned, the disgusting pigs could go on strike and never return. Of the two women in the office, Lenore, the unmarried one, was the target of frequent ass-pinching and lewd jokes. Most of the drivers leered at her in a way that made her feel undressed and filthy. She endured innumerable racist references, with some of the truckers calling crows "nigger-chickens" and slandering the handful of black drivers behind their backs. While not intended for her, the comments pierced her heart. She chewed the insides of her mouth in an attempt not to respond. She had retorted only once and the drivers retaliated by leaving used condoms in her desk drawer. But for two sympathetic drivers who got the offensive co-workers off her back, she almost quit.

Lenore jumped up from the couch, punching the TV power off. She needed air. Now. Her shoes made their way back onto her feet. Determined to stay away from the house for as long as possible, she decided she would eat out. She zippered an extra twenty into her sweat jacket pocket and flew out the door.

Making her way back to the Mud River park, she forced herself to walk, though her breath refused to slow. She headed north. A small wooden bridge spanned a slough. Lenore stopped and leaned on a rough rail, looking into the leaf-clogged murk below. Her knot fluttered like a trapped bird. She spotted a frog, its rubbery chin silently pulsating. The afternoon sun winked through gaps in the aspen leaves overhead. In the fall, the leaves shook, rattling like beans in a gourd. Too soft and young for that, today they chattered in hushed tones.

Of three paths beyond the bridge, Lenore's feet followed the middle one. Normally, she veered left and walked the lower route on the river's edge. Today, she climbed the hill to the Mud River Cemetery, her shoes slipping on rotten mulch. The exertion forced her breathing to deepen. She pushed open a cast-iron, curlicued gate which was set into a cyclone fence. The gate and fence were incongruous bedfellows, an attempt by the city council to beautify (if one could call cyclone fences beautiful) the cemetery for tourists while maintaining a sense of history. At the time the fence was erected, the council had most of the trees ripped from the grounds, all except those along the ridge of a bluff that afforded a glorious view of the river. The lack of trees allowed the caretaker to mow without spinning round and round on his lawn tractor. With no protective shade, the sun crisped the grass into dormancy by peak summer and the mower became unnecessary.

A wind gust brushed Lenore's hair and face as she entered the cemetery. It was commonly known that the cemetery was windy, even when the air was calm in the rest of the city. The spirits of the interred supposedly caused the phenomenon.

Lenore was drawn by a rhythmic thunking on the headstone of Stefan Gower. His metal military service marker twisted back and forth, hitting the polished black granite. *What are you trying to tell me, Colonel Gower?* she thought as she studied his stone. She liked to play this game, using epitaphs to puzzle out the lives of the people buried beneath her feet. Did these final reductive words do justice to the essence of a person? Date born. Date dead. A prescriptive family role. Wife, mother, sister, daughter. Husband, father, brother, son. Long lived or cut short. If there was enough money for etching, prayers for a heavenly afterlife might be offered, or a poem or quote. Above all, the interred were beloved. Even the royal bastards were loved by someone, if not in life, then in death. Trespasses faded and could be forgiven. Six or more feet of earth and a cement vault helped to soften a person's past misdeeds.

Viewed from above, Lenore zigged and zagged about the graveyard, sampling markers the way a honeybee tastes

started toward the big machine, curious about how a grave looked before it was draped with the accoutrements of death; the coffin-lowering hydraulic mechanism and the artificial turf. One mustn't touch a dead body or even dirt from the grave. Mortality might rub off.

On her way to the backhoe, Lenore noticed a jardinière filled with a dozen pink roses. Surprised that the flowers were real, she stopped to smell them. The scent was strong and fresh, the blossoms scarcely open. Rarely were this many long-stemmed roses left for the dead. Carnations, mums, lilacs, marigolds, perhaps. Something inexpensive where it mattered not if they were stolen. But roses? Lenore read the stone to find out who warranted such affection. Grace Clark. She had died a-year-and-a-half ago. She was only 41, Lenore's age . . . . Lenore's age.

Unbidden, a sob wrenched itself free from Lenore's chest, the knot shattering with the primal sound. She dropped to her knees and slammed her fists into the ground, pummeling Grace Clark's grave with rage. "God damn it!" Thoughts wrestled with each other in her brain, struggling to be the first to pop into her consciousness. "I hate my house! I hate my job! I hate my parents for leaving me! God! I hate my life!" Tears flooded her eyes, drenching her cheeks and dripping onto the grass below. She didn't wipe them away. Instead, she got up and ran . . . ran toward the open grave by the backhoe.

She didn't care who saw her, this lunatic escaped from the asylum of propriety. She shook her fists at the sky and cursed as she ran. She would throw herself into the grave. No one would miss her if she broke her neck. Absolutely no one would miss her.

As she approached the hole, she stopped short, peering in. Dear God. It was a long way down. She wasn't sure she was ready to be extinct. Lenore the dodo.

Still sniveling, she wiped her nose on her tank top and sat on the edge, her legs dangling. Air entered her lungs in uneven snorts. Picturing herself in the bottom of the hole, she shuddered and fresh tears arose. There was so much she wanted to do. Her life had derailed when her parents found their way to early graves and she had never gotten it back on the tracks.

"Damn! I've wasted my life. I'm not teaching. I didn't graduate. I'm stuck in that rotten house and this crappy town. My job sucks, sucks, sucks! I'm a complete failure!" She wailed and hammered her thighs with frustration coursing full force through her hands.

Worn from the sudden burst, she reclined with her legs still hanging in the hole and covered her eyes with her hands. "Why hasn't anyone ever given me roses?" She had always intended to fall in love, get married, have babies, but here she was . . . an Old Maid. An Old Maid in a sucky job with jerky-ass men who were creepy and insensitive, unlike dead Grace's husband. Who else would've left roses? Her stomach quivered as she realized that she was unloved. And that meant that she was most certainly unlovable. A failure and unlovable. She wept with the finality of it all. Unwilling to give up on life, yet as unwanted as ABC gum, she cried until she fell asleep.

Moments later, she woke, her body depleted from the storm of tears. Advice from her father crystallized in her mind. He had once told her, "Lenore, when you're between a rock and a hard place, move the rock." It seemed so easy. "Move the rock," she said with conviction. She sat up, pulled her legs from the grave, stood and dusted off her butt and hands.

From this point in the cemetery, she looked north and could see the Mud River Flats and the Tin Man's house just below her. She strode through the cemetery gate and down the hill. It was time to visit her father's friend, Tom. She hadn't seen him in years, but now was a good time. She didn't question why this was a good time or why Tom. It was imperative. When Abner St. Cyr tells you something, you listen. So, off she went, to Blue Street and Tom's Bar as the Tin Man hammered freshly flattened pop cans onto his house.

Thinking. He couldn't get away from it. Couldn't detach his mind from his head. Or, maybe his mind was in his ass. It felt like it some days. Hell, most days. Sully shifted on his barstool. If his mind was in his ass, he needed to give it some air. The black vinyl seat was molding to his bottom and making him sweat.

The barstool, this particular one, was at the end of the bar, as far as one could get from the front door. No need to ruin a perfectly good buzz by exposing it to fresh air and sunlight. Sully, however, was nowhere near the blissful, unthinking state. He'd only been planted on his barstool for an hour and expected to remain several more.

And the barstool, this particular one, was most assuredly Sully's. Woe be to anyone who snatched it before Sully arrived. It had happened a few times, before Sully had quite established his routine. When he saw a woman on the stool, he was miffed, but didn't think it gentlemanly to displace her, and so took another stool. It wasn't the same. He couldn't get comfortable on the new stool because it didn't allow him to scope out the entire room. He left early in a huff that day.

On a later occasion, Sully had gone to the Men's Room. When he returned, he found a pseudo-cowboy, all shiny buckle, white hat, unscuffed pointy black boots and bolo tie, on his stool. The manicure exposed him for what he really was, a play-acting business man. However, the costume lent him a very real swagger and when informed that this stool was the special domain of Sullivan Henry Clark, the buffed and even nails were carefully tucked within the cowboy's fist as it was rammed into the bridge of Sully's nose.

Because Sully was an afternoon regular, Tom, the bar-keep, took pity on him and kept a "Reserved" sign ready for the stool. If Sully had been a prime-time regular, Tom would've made him fend for himself, or kicked him out for any trouble caused by his territorial behavior. A guy's gotta make a living, after all. Sully understood this.

It was better this way, being an afternoon regular. He arrived every day around two and stayed until about eight, leaving before the bar rush. He preferred the dark quiet of a dead bar. Other than the occasional delivery man and Tom, there was a congenial lack of people. No loud-mouthed drunks rambling and repeating themselves. No young ladies masquerading as demure strumpets. They dared men to look at their stylishly messy hair, sultry mascara, succulent lips, and clingy, transparent blouses with dangerously low necklines. If a man took the dare and the girl wasn't drunk enough, he'd be damned to the kingdom where men became pigs. If the tease was blotto, she'd practically climb into his lap and be ready to do him right there on the bar-stool.

When he'd been a prime-timer, Sully had often been the target of this behavior. Though his dark hair was reced-ing and he had a bit of a gut, he was aware that an aura of attractiveness remained about him. The blessing of genetics allowed him a youthful face for a forty-year-old. While he looked about ten years younger, his maturity and politeness sent a signal to women that spoke of steadiness and commit-ment. Cute and no ring. (They always checked.) Definitely marriage material. What better musk could a man emit? Al-though girls these days seemed to appreciate their conquest of men over matrimony with them.

Nope, Sully was glad he had switched to afternoons. Of

course, he'd had a little help in his decision. Several DWIs resulted in a lost license. Buses stopped running at 10 p.m. He thought cabs were a rip-off. His house was too far away to make walking practical. By adding up the variables, he had reached the solution. Instead of closing down the bar, he'd get here earlier and leave in enough time to catch the bus. Then he wouldn't have to deal with barstool interlopers and embarrassing female ardor. He was sure Grace would approve of his logic. She wouldn't like the whiskey plates he'd have on the pickup when he finally got his license back, but there was nothing he could do about that. He could hear her tongue clucking at him and took a hard gulp of beer in order to shake the noise.

Sully continued his appraisal of the afternoon bar scene. The haze of cigarette smoke, while stubbornly clinging to the air, was at least bearable. When Sully had changed his schedule, he discovered that he felt less hungover. It definitely wasn't the alcohol. He still drank just as much, three-to-four piss-colored American beers per hour chased by several shots of whiskey at the end of his bar stint. His nose eventually gave him the answer. When he awoke in the mornings following his early bar schedule, he found that his nostrils were not as snuffly as they had been with the late-night schedule. His head was clearer and less achy. Oxygen seemed to serve as a partial antidote to that scruffy hang-dog morning-after feeling. Less alcohol would help, but that wasn't an option.

Instead of the usual cacophony of a digital jukebox plus three televisions tuned to different stations, only the TV above the bar was on. Tom liked to watch the news as he inventoried the liquor. He alternated between stations to get opposing views on the same story. Sometimes he turned on C-SPAN so he and Sully could chuckle over legislative pomposity and filibustering.

Just now there was a story on about a Greenville boy. Greenville, population 26,333, give or take. Not huge by any standards, but big enough to have decent shopping and not know everyone.

'Course, as chance would have it, Sully did know this boy, or of him at any rate. He belonged to Emanuel Dobbs, one of his former carpenters. The guy didn't do much. He put all his faith in God and figured that if he were devout enough, God would come down out of the sky, skillfully swinging a hammer and finish framing up the two-by-fours Emanuel stared at much of the day. Sully kept telling him that God had invented the air-nailer so as to spread the work out a bit. It was important for human beings to take on these smaller tasks, like building houses, so that God was free for the really big stuff like love and death and disasters and the apocalypse.

Emanuel was sure he'd be one of the chosen few to be transported to heaven during the End Times. He had accepted Jesus as his personal Lord and Savior and he was saved, just like that. Sully didn't put much stock in it. If anyone deserved a spot in heaven, it was his Grace, not Emanuel, the lazy bag of hot wind.

Emanuel's boy, Monroe, poor kid. He'd been born odd. Didn't talk when a toddler should. He clicked and buzzed and cackled, with nary an intelligible word slipping out until he was six or seven. Emanuel and his wife, Becky, did their best to keep him out of sight. Monroe was an embarrassment to their sin-free family. He smacked too much of punishment bathed in the fires of Hell, which countered their view of their own goodness and salvation. They simply didn't deserve this damaged child.

Their opinion of the boy changed when they discovered his gift. All that nonsensical noise he made could be directed toward healing people.

Sully had considered taking Grace to see Monroe, but she wouldn't hear of it. She refused to take advantage of the boy, something his parents did aplenty. Emanuel and Becky, seeing the money-making potential of their son, had secured a manager for him and scheduled grueling healing sessions at their church. Like an organ grinder's leashed monkey,

Monroe sat for hours each day at Baptized in Christ Evangelical Church speaking in tongues at the busloads of people streaming in from around the country who were seeking to be healed, whether from a hangnail or a brain tumor.

Monroe's manager was certainly capable. What with all the media attention, the membership rolls of Baptized in Christ swelled. Donations were always accepted and the money poured in from the gratefully healed. Sully was pretty sure that Monroe didn't see much of it. The church, the manager, and Emanuel and Becky, however, were more than materially set for the apocalypse. 'Course, they kept quiet about it. Their story, and they were sticking to it, was that they were just doing God's work by giving Monroe to the sick.

Sully snorted and took a swig of his drink. Fat lot of good a pile of money, a giant house, and a gazillion baubles would do during the rapture. He laughed when he remembered that the saved are ripped from their clothes and, thus, go to heaven naked. What would Emanuel think of that?

Tom heard Sully's snicker and raised his Andy Rooney eyebrows as he placed clean glasses underneath the bar. "What's so funny?" he asked. He rarely heard Sully laugh.

"Nothing, nothing," said Sully. "Say, could you give me another?" He pushed his empty can toward Tom.

"No problem," said Tom. He popped the tab before handing the beer to Sully. "So, how's it going?"

"Same 's yesterday . . . okay. This is my excitement for the day," replied Sully.

"Looking at my ugly mug is your excitement for the day? You need to get a life, my friend," said Tom.

"Not much to get a life for." Sully glanced up to the high shelf along the mirrored back wall of the bar. He avoided looking at his reflection. He felt creepy catching his own eyes and watching his every move. Instead, he focused on the bottles lining the shelf. Some of them contained up-turned ships, resting on their sterns in an impossible sailing position. Interspersed with the bottles containing ships were

corked bottles with rolled paper inside. The corks were unnecessary as these messages-in-bottles were dry docked.

"Get any new messages?" said Sully.

"Not since the last time you asked." Tom reached up to
pull a cobalt blue wine bottle from the middle of the shelf.
"Did I ever show you the one B.B. King wrote?"

"About a million times," said Sully.

So as not to waste the motion, Tom examined the bottle
and dusted it with a bar rag before returning it to its spot.

"Know anybody famous coming to town who'd like to
add to my collection?" he asked Sully.

"Well, you could see if our own *cause célèbre* would write
you a message," said Sully.

"The kid? The one who speaks in tongues?" said Tom.

"That's the one. Monroe Dobbs. 'Course, now it could
be a little difficult, what with his disappearing," said Sully.

"Too bad about that," said Tom. "I hope they find him
soon. Scary world out there."

"Yeah. It sure is. I'd hate to be raising kids now," said
Sully.

Tom was about to reply in the affirmative when the
door opened and a young man dressed in a striped, button-
down shirt emblazoned with the name of a liquor company
entered. Instead, he excused himself and took the man into
the office behind the bar in order to privately conduct business.

After Tom and the young man disappeared, the door
reopened and a woman, silhouetted by the late afternoon
sun, teetered at the threshold. A moment's hesitation later,
she stepped through.

As the door closed, her shadow-self gave way to flesh
and details. Sully didn't recognize her. Pretty, though.
Something about her reminded him of Grace. Except, Grace
had blonde hair and this woman was a brunette. *Was it
her figure?* thought Sully. Sort of, but not really. Grace was
slimmer.

Sully attempted to pin down the resemblance as the

woman's eyes flicked to adjust to the low light. She perched
at the edge of the barstool nearest to the door, as far from
Sully as possible. She shot a glance and a half-grin at Sully,
who raised his beer can to her. Quickly, she looked away
and appeared as ready to take flight from her stool as a bird
being stalked by a twitchy cat. She absently picked up a
white square bar napkin and rolled it between her fingers.

Despite the uncertainty that lingered about her, Sully
sensed resolve. She might worry the napkin into oblivion
and startle at the slightest provocation, but she was determined to stay as long as needed. Maybe she was here to
milk a donation out of Tom. Plenty of charities out there
wanted a hand-out. By the looks of her, it was obvious that
she wasn't used to asking for money, or being in a bar, for
that matter.

Fingers snapped in Sully's brain. *The tracksuit. That's
it,* he thought. Grace never bothered to dress up when she
was out. Comfortable clothes. No makeup. Forget skirts
and heels. Grace was a no-frills gal who laughed at the
thought of trying to impress anyone. When she was in her
pottery studio, she wore denim bib overalls and a bright
t-shirt. If she had to go into town for some reason, she'd
wear her artist's uniform out of the house, never mind the
splatters of clay or the hair straggling out from underneath
her red paisley dew rag. On occasion, when she wanted to
feel clean, she'd shower and don a coordinated tracksuit and
tank top, much like the gray one this woman had on.

Sully's heart panged. Another swallow of beer didn't
erase the image of Grace from his mind. He could see her
through the French doors of her studio when he got home
from work. She'd be hunched over her wheel, slumping and
forming the clay as rock music rattled the windows. Always
she sang, her voice sliding over words she did not know.
He'd stare in at her, amazed that anyone could be so happy,
her happiness so infectious that his meanest self slipped
away and he'd want to join her.

God, she was sexy in her bibs. He'd try to sneak up

behind her, but somehow she always knew he was there. She'd pretend, for the sake of the game, that he wasn't in the room. It drove her wild when he grabbed her, brushed the hair from the nape of her neck and planted tens of tiny kisses there. He'd drink in her scent, wet clay and lavendar. Her knees would go weak and she'd demand to be carried to the bedroom, but not before they'd gotten tipsy from sharing a full-tongued kiss. After making love, he'd tell her dirty jokes in bed. She'd play comedic straight man, acting offended and trying not to laugh, until she could hold it no more and her twinkling voice burst forth.

Sully shook his head and downed the last half of his beer. Why couldn't he forget? No, not forget. He didn't want to forget Grace. He just wanted relief from the pain of losing her. Still, he needed to move on. She would have wanted that. It'd been over a year, for Christ's sake. Time enough to pull himself up by his bootstraps, quit pickling himself in alcohol. Death would be better than this half-life composed of the construction business and Tom's Bar. He'd be with her, wherever she was.

Grace was shaking her finger at him, as she did every time he sunk into lament. She knew him so well that when she was diagnosed, she made him promise that he would take care of himself after her death. Under stress, he tended to skip vital life rituals like eating, bathing, and paying bills. Even in death, Grace kept him going, kept him putting one foot in front of the other. He moved through his hollow days, keeping his word, tempting though it was to break it. Many an afternoon he sat in the dusty rocking chair in her studio, choking down a sandwich. And she stood there, clucking, always clucking, and telling him that he needed to eat. It was not his time yet and she didn't want him to turn to dust and blow away. After his tasteless lunch, he'd grab a bottle of whiskey, and go to the living room. Thankfully, Grace didn't make him promise to quit drinking.

On Tuesdays, flowers joined him for his routine. Following work, he'd pick up a dozen pink roses from Lilac

& Finches and take them home. The roses had to be pink. Red roses reminded Grace of vials of blood and she hated blood. He arranged the flowers as best he could in a large cut crystal vase on the glass-topped coffee table, never minding if the thorns pricked him. As he filled a shot glass, he'd remember how they used to lounge together on the couch, he sipping whiskey, she a steaming lemon-mint tea. In those days, he only needed one drink.

After conjuring memories of Grace, Sully went to Tom's Bar, as usual, then returned to the house to sit vigil with the roses in the half-lit living room. Several more shots made comfortable companions and coaxed him into an undreaming stupor.

On Wednesday mornings, with muscles cramped from sleeping crookedly, Sully hobbled the roses, *sans* vase, to the Mud River Cemetery and left them for Grace.

Where was Tom, damn it? He needed another drink. The woman who triggered his mope had torn up several napkins and was piling them on the bar's surface. He hated her for it. The mope, not the napkins. Hell, yes, the napkins! Why'd she have to make a mess of his bar?

Just then, she looked up, her gaze locking with his and, pointing to the shredded napkins, she mouthed, "Sorry," as if she had read his mind.

Sully cleared his throat, more to choke back his emotions than for any accumulated mucus. The woman's resemblance to Grace ran deeper than her outfit.

Tom and the liquor distributor returned from the back room, their business finished on a handshake. As the young man left, Tom spotted the woman. His eyes sparkled and he danced a little two-step over to her. He smiled so broadly that Sully thought his false teeth might slip out.

"Well, I'll be King of the Fish Squeezers!" boomed Tom. "It's my Lolly-Bean!

The woman shrugged her eyes on behalf of her shoulders, which were restrained in Tom's trap-like hug. Her expression apologized to Sully for the ridiculous nickname.

Tom released her and held her at arm's length, examining her as a jeweler might study an exquisite emerald.

"How've you been, Lenore? I haven't seen you in forever," said Tom.

"Well . . . okay," she said.

Sully, who was concentrating on his empty can and trying unsuccessfully not to eavesdrop, heard something more in the pause than silence. Sadness settled there like a stone in the bed of an ancient river.

"Dad sent me," said Lenore.

"Have you been seeing ghosts like Old Lady Fortune used to?" asked Tom.

Sully could relate.

"Old Lady Fortune?" said Lenore, sidetracked from her original line of thinking. "Was she Clotilda Fortune? I was up at the cemetery and saw her grave. I imagined she read crystal balls."

"She did that, too," said Tom. "Spooky, that one. Dressed all in black. Had a dowager's hump. Made every effort to look like a witch, just like her grandmother, but she was the sweetest thing. Couldn't stop by her house without her feeding you. Neighborhood kids always hung out there. Weren't scared of her in the least."

"She sounds interesting," said Lenore.

"She was. But, I digress, as usual. So, your father sent you?"

"Yeah. It's not like I saw him or anything, but I had this sense that he wanted me to talk to you, so here I am," said Lenore. "Sounds silly, doesn't it?"

"Not at all, child," said Tom. "Your father was a smart man. If he told you to come, he had a reason. Let's see if we can figure out what it is."

Sully cleared his throat and shifted on his stool.

Tom turned in his direction and said, "Forgive me, Sully. Can I get you another drink?"

"That'd be nice," said Sully, trying to keep the sarcasm from his voice. *It's becoming Apology Central in here*, he thought.

As Tom retrieved a beer for Sully, he beckoned Lenore to the other end of the bar. "C'mon over and meet my friend, Sully," he said.

Lenore hopped off her stool and walked to Sully's post.

"Sullivan Clark, this is Lenore St. Cyr," said Tom. "Lenore, this is Sully."

"Pleased to meet you," said Lenore.

As they shook on it, Sully warily replied, "Same here."

Simultaneously, the two looked away from each other, unsure of what to say next.

"Pull up a stool, Lolly. Make yourself comfortable," said Tom. He poured a soda and set the glass in front of her. "It's on the house."

"Thanks, but you know I'm more than old enough for a beer, Tom," laughed Lenore, as she shoved the glass back to him.

"Right. It's hard to believe you're all grown up," said Tom. He got her a beer and a fresh glass.

The phone rang. Tom said, "I'll take that in the office. You two make yourselves acquainted."

Sully watched from the corner of his eye as Lenore made a ritual of slowly pouring her beer into the tipped glass, avoiding the production of a foamy head. She raised the glass and saluted him in the mirror before taking a delicate sip. He returned cheers with his can and slugged some of the cold liquid down. He turned to face her, not willing to have a conversation with her reflection.

"How long have you known Tom?" he asked.

"Since I was a kid. Isn't it obvious?" she said.

"Geez, I was just asking."

"Look, I didn't mean to snap. I've had kind of a bad day, well, bad life, really, and I was hoping Tom could help."

"He certainly helps me, as long as he keeps these coming," said Sully, gesturing to his drink.

"That's not the sort of help I need."

Sully thought, *Touchy, touchy*, as he stared at her chest

and wondered how she might look skinny dipping in the river. If he could just stroke them . . . . Holy crap! His censor woke up and stopped his roaming mind. Lenore was blushing. Sully, embarrassed by his sophomoric behavior, felt an apology of his own forming. It wasn't like him to be distracted this way.

He looked into Lenore's eyes and was surprised to see Grace's irises, gray with blue flecks. Only Grace wasn't scolding him, rather, she was encouraging him. "Go on," she was saying, like a mother urging her toddler into a wading pool.

He shook his head and refocused. Same eyes, but bemused, apparently wondering what was going through his mind.

She startled him with her next comment.

"Do you like monkeys?" Lenore asked.

"Never thought much about 'em," he said.

"Why don't you come with me to the zoo, then? Let's see what you think," said Lenore. She got up from the stool and gently tugged his arm.

Grace whispered in his ear, "You're a fool if you don't go," and he got up, too, forgetting the half-finished beer.

As they left Tom's Bar, they saw the Tin Man outside, violin case open. Lenore pulled a twenty-dollar bill out of her pocket and threw it into the case. Though they were too preoccupied to see the gesture, the Tin Man winked at Lenore and Sully as they walked down the sidewalk.

Tongues

Monroe Dobbs sat under the table, his knees pulled to his chest, his arms wrapped tightly around his shins. He rocked and clicked. The table, which sat in a corner of his bedroom, was round and wooden and worn and was covered with a blanket. Monroe had been under it for three days and showed no signs of surrendering his post. His flanks were protected by the walls behind him.

He just had to keep them out, which was pretty easy. They were scared of him, or rather, of his voice. If anyone tried to lift the blanket, he snarled and grumbled, growling from the back of his throat, allowing the noises to vibrate from the pit of his stomach. This voice was enough to frighten the dead and that's why they were scared.

He didn't care. He'd sit here as long as he had to. It was time for him to get his way for once. He had put up with their shit long enough. He was sixteen – certainly old enough to make his own decisions. Especially concerning his voice. He rolled his tongue, burring.

They all thought he was stupid. "We'll see who's stupid," he muttered. He wasn't going back to church until they met his demands. Nope. No more healings. No matter how pitifully they begged, or how much their sores oozed, or how close to death they imagined themselves to be.

"Nope, nope, nope, nope, nope, nope," he repeated in rhythm. "Nope, nope, nope, stupid, nope, nope, nope, stupid." He tapped his forefinger in time on the floor. As the word 'stupid' reverberated in his head, a growl rose again, but he stifled it as it reached his throat and it came out as a gurgly teeth gnashing.

"Stupid! How double-damn dare they treat me as stupid!" The indignation spun inside, mixing with thoughts that maybe they were right -- he really was stupid -- but he crossed out these negative thoughts and was left with the original indignation. "Just because they can't understand me doesn't make me stupid. It makes them stupid!"

He mentally removed his sisters from the general con-demnation. Jenna and Brittany understood him. They had known what he was saying long before he could talk in the conventional sense of the word.

He remembered the time his mom was feeding him in the high chair. He could see the stove across the room, but she couldn't because she was facing him. His father inadvertently threw a blue and white striped towel on the stove before leaving the kitchen. The burner was still hot and the towel smoldered. He could hear the heat snaking and searing its way through the fibers of the towel, which cringed in an effort to get away. He squawked like a blue jay to warn his mother, who took no notice of the drama behind her. Instead, she seemed surprised by his outburst and tried to shush him. This only made him screech louder. He was communicating with her, telling her what was happening, but she wasn't getting it. Jenna, who was five at the time, had entered the room upon hearing Monroe and, before catching sight of the smoking towel, said, "Mom, he's trying to tell you something," at which point his mother's nostrils flared with the scent of burnt cloth. She turned, grabbed the towel by an unsinged corner and tossed it into the sink, dowsing the charred thing with cold water.

When Monroe later recalled the incident for Jenna, she was amazed. She told him that he was only six months old at the time, a very early age for holding fast a memory with such accuracy. It was sign of high intelligence, she said, which relieved Monroe. Because of the language barrier, he had assumed that he was a human being of average intelligence who'd been born into a group of retarded people.

Monroe stretched his cramped legs. They poked out from under the blanket. His parakeet, Cricket, saw the movement and chirped. The bird wanted to play. Monroe chittered back, an edge of impatience sneaking into his reply. When Cricket responded with disappointment, Monroe explained that he would make it up to him when he wasn't feeling so frustrated. Cricket took it well and was silent. Monroe returned to mulling all that had led up to his present situation. He tick-tocked while he sifted through the events of his life.

He'd been colicky for several months after his birth, or so everyone had thought. Monroe knew better. His stomach wasn't distressing him, it was all the noise. So many sounds, even the tiniest, thumped his eardrums and coursed through his body, driving him to angry tears. He couldn't sort them all out and the cacophony overwhelmed him.

Not only was his hearing super sensitive – he could pick up the rough scratching of a fly rubbing its legs across a room – colors gave off their own noises, as did people. He'd had to learn to focus on the sounds he wanted to hear and filter out those he didn't. By the time he was three months old, he had reasonably mastered this skill and found that everything was speaking to him. The pale blue curtains in his room whispered, "Swoosh, swoosh, shh," and sung him to sleep. Dusty brown potatoes hummed low, like stately Tibetan monks. The rocking chair in the living room complained about its loose, creaky joints. Fluorescent lights screamed violent pink at him.

These languages spoke more elementally than words and were easier to learn than English. They were honest languages that bounced off his diaphragm and told him who he could trust and who he couldn't.

When he spoke in pure sound, he picked the language that was most appropriate for the situation. Thus, when there was danger, he shrieked like a blue jay. In a case of accidental intuition, his parents had given him Jay as a middle name, but the irony was lost on them.

Unfortunately, the language that was most appropriate for him led to confused looks and exasperation from his parents. He babbled and chattered incessantly as he grew, partially to communicate with them, partially to filter some of the external noise. When he could see that he wasn't getting through to them, he'd find Jenna and have her translate. Like most translators, she sometimes skewed his original meaning, but it was close enough for his purposes. Brittany, two years his junior, was even better than Jenna at interpreting his many languages. He would sit in front of her baby seat and entertain her with a multitude of sounds such that she learned what he was saying and could speak back to him.

By the time Monroe was three, his parents were embarrassed by his lack of proper speech and dragged him to a good number of specialists, none of whom could ascertain his acute hearing. When he was five and still not speaking, his parents figured he was a lost cause and didn't bother to start him on the home school curriculum that Jenna was working her way through. Jenna, appalled that they were so insensitive, pestered them to try, but they refused. So, she took it upon herself to teach Monroe the basics of English.

Around this time, they stopped taking him out in public. He could hear the tones of shame that pulsed through his parents' underlying body sounds. His father, Emanuel, whose name was so lyrical, had a body sound that was lazy and sly. Lyrical in its own noxious way, it went slicka, slicka, slicka. In contrast, his mother Becky had a vaguely kindhearted, but easily confused body sound – tweetle, tweetle, tweetle – interrupted by static – ksh, ksh, ksssh. She gladly followed Emanuel's lead in all of life's decisions. When Monroe's father regularly referred to him as "The Idiot" in front of others, she did not disagree.

It wasn't until he was almost seven and speaking in

words that Monroe realized that other people didn't hear what he was hearing. He explained his experiences to Jenna, who checked some books out of the library and together they discovered he was synesthetic. His finely tuned hearing was not without precedent, either. Nikola Tesla, the scientist who harnessed alternating current, had had the same ability.

Monroe stretched his arms as much as he was able under the table and held the image of Jenna in his mind's eye. He could hear her body sound, efficient and loving and seeking fairness: Ta-ta te-ta-toe, ta-ta te-ta-toe. He missed her. She'd know how to help him, but she was off at college. Because she was normal, she got to have a life. He didn't.

He cried then. He was so tired, exhausted really, by spending hour upon hour, days upon days, at Baptized in Christ Church. For almost three years now, his parents and manager had booked him for six days a week, seven hours a day. The usual time ran from one in the afternoon until eight in the evening. No healings were scheduled for Sundays because that was a church day, after all.

Each day Monroe faced long lines of desperate people. They all wanted to be whole again. Monroe was happy to give them this, but they never stopped coming, their misery unending. Sure, those he was able to heal were overjoyed, but he couldn't heal everyone. The failure niggled at his psyche.

Through his tears, Monroe heard, "Slicka slick, slicka slick, slicka slick, slicka slick." His thoughts and tears froze. His father was coming down the hall, toward his door.

Emanuel turned the knob, gently opened the door, entered, and quietly stood in front of Monroe's sanctuary.

There was no hiding his true mood from Monroe, who covered his ears to block the rage booming off his father. Emanuel's anger crashed to the floor and shot under the edge of the blanket, striking Monroe like shrapnel.

"Are you ready to come out from under that table, son?" Emanuel said as he tried to maintain his composure.

Monroe kept still, barely breathing.

"God damn it! Answer me!" Emanuel pounded the top of the table, his actions now matching his body sound. "I don't care what kind of power you have, you will show me some respect."

Emanuel was mistaken if he thought he could scare Monroe into submission. When fear of this magnitude entered Monroe's body, it roused his instincts and he unconsciously reacted to his circumstances through a suitable language. Taking on the characteristics of a pit bull in attack mode, he snarled back, "No, sir!"

This mix of anger and fear persuaded his father to back away from the table. As he retreated out the door, he shouted, "Fine, Monroe. Have it your way. You'll get nothing more to eat until you get your ass out from under there."

Monroe mumbled, "Go to hell!" and waited until his father's footsteps receded. Then he slid out from under the table, quick as a lizard, and carefully shut the door. Before Cricket could tweet, he was back in his original position, knees to his chest, rocking and clicking to calm himself.

"He doesn't get it, he just doesn't get it," said Monroe and he cried again. "I can't keep doing this." He grabbed a corner of the blanket and wiped his eyes. The blanket, a dull green wool-blend, scratched and didn't soak up the tears, but it sounded nice. It gave off a mellow oooma lama tone.

Monroe thought, I *could hurt him if I wanted to. That'd show him.*

All he had to do was create dissonance in his father's body sound. Make the right noise and Emanuel's cells would go haywire in whatever manner Monroe chose – reproduce crazily, eat themselves, shut down. But it wasn't in Monroe to harm his father. Aside from the tremendous guilt he would inevitably feel, he couldn't tolerate the chaotic sounds produced when illness clashed with smooth-flowing healthy body sounds.

Healing arose by counteracting the chaos, reversing the process. When sick people came to him, Monroe could hone in on specific disturbances in their body sounds and, using the correct tones, he could settle the disorder and bring bodies back into harmony. He enjoyed making bodies sing.

His mom called what he did speaking in tongues. She was the first to witness his ability. They had lived in a different house then, a smaller one on Brown Street, on the west side of the Mud River. Sliding glass doors opened out to a backyard that was overgrown around the edges. A dog house sat on an island of grass surrounded by a moat of dirt. King, the Dobbs family's long-haired, mottled mutt, paced on his chain and had worried the circular patch until it was as solid as concrete.

Monroe, who was thirteen at the time, sat at the dining room table, half studying math, half observing life outside the doors. He caught a whirring sound and ducked. Whoomp! A robin flew into the glass and dropped to the ground. Monroe jumped up and was instantly out the door. King barked as Monroe knelt by the stunned bird. The robin panted through its beak. One wing was spread and cocked and Monroe could hear that it was broken. His mother had come to the door to investigate King's commotion.

"Don't touch that bird, Monroe!" she said. "It won't make it with its wing like that." She added, "You'll probably catch something."

Monroe motioned for her to stay quiet while he murmured and burbled at the bird. Once he fixed the wing, he gently cradled the bird between his palms and continued his soothing coo until the robin recovered and flew away.

He looked up at his mom and found her mouth agape. Her tweetling and kssh-ing cycled at a faster frequency, a frequency of astonishment. She said nothing at that moment, but went back inside the house. Later, he heard her recounting the healing to his father.

"Really, Emanuel, the wing was broken. Monroe, he spoke in tongues and the bird was fine."

"Now, Becky, I'm sure the wing wasn't as bad as it looked. Birds hit windows and go into shock all the time. It takes a few minutes for them to recover. That's all," he said.

"Besides, that boy is always talking nonsense."

"I know what I saw," she replied, but her static increased as she spoke and Monroe could tell that Emanuel had replaced certainty with doubt.

Emanuel's incredulity didn't last long. Within a month of the robin incident, while Emanuel was walking King, another dog attacked, ripping a deep gash in King's hip along with leaving other bloody wounds. Emanuel carried King back to the house.

During the flurry of his mother grabbing hot water and old bath towels and his father phoning the vet, Monroe settled in next to King and chanted low, long syllables. His father paused during his conversation with the vet and watched Monroe. He almost dropped the receiver when he saw King's injuries zip up and disappear.

Monroe could hear the vet saying, "Hello? Hello? Mr. Dobbs, are you there?"

"Dad, the vet's talking to you," he said.

Emanuel shook himself from his daze and resumed his conversation with, "Dr. Goodwin? Yeah, yeah, I'm here. You are never going to believe this . . . I can hardly believe it myself, but I just saw it with my own two eyes. King is fine now, thanks to Monroe."

He went on to explain, and explain again, to the vet how King was healed by Monroe. It was the first time Monroe felt any measure of pride aimed at him by his father and he cherished the moment. There had not been many more like it since.

Dr. Goodwin paid the Dobbs' household a visit that evening to see King's miraculous recovery. A fine scar was all that was left of the gash. Because Dr. Goodwin hadn't been present, he couldn't wrap his mind around the events described by Emanuel and Becky. He was curious, though, and asked Monroe to come to the clinic the next day. He watched as over and over Monroe healed his many furry and feathered patients. No matter what the diagnosis, as long as the animal wasn't too far gone, Monroe was able to cure the ailment, all through sounds specifically chosen for the particular patient's circumstances. Dr. Goodwin knew that sound waves could be used to break up gallstones, but he had never seen anything like this. He suggested that Emanuel and Becky take their son to the state university to be studied. They had other ideas.

Emanuel figured that if Monroe could heal animals, surely he could heal human beings. He tested his theory on Jenna and Brittany. When the girls suffered minor cuts, Monroe was allowed to work his magic on them. After Brittany stepped on a rusty nail in the yard, Monroe's voice swooped over the hole in her foot. The sound brought the blood to the surface in order to clean the wound before Monroe closed it. Following Monroe's realignment and knitting of the broken clavicle Jenna received during a softball game, with before and after X-rays to confirm the phenomenon, Emanuel had all the proof he needed. He knew that people would pay any price to be well. If he could set up healing sessions, perhaps at church, and get the word out about Monroe's talent, there'd be no end to the riches he'd acquire.

With this sketch of a plan, Emanuel decided to hire a manager for Monroe. Enter Sheldon Rhodes. He was all business; his body sound snapping like heels on saluting military boots.

Sheldon arranged everything with the church. He rounded up some ailing Greenville residents and scheduled a meeting with church elders so that Monroe could demonstrate his ability.

When the elders were assured that the church would get a cut in the profits and not be held liable for any problems arising from healing sessions, they agreed. Monroe often saw these elders gathered in a front corner of the church while he was working. As they stood watching the throngs, he noted that their eyes sparkled. They periodically rubbed their palms and shared quiet congratulatory remarks. Emanuel often joined these men, whose posture made Monroe queasy.

Once there was an agreement with the church, Sheldon saw to it that all legal angles were covered. Contracts between Sheldon, Monroe's parents, and Baptized in Christ Church were signed. Release forms were drawn up for patients. No, not patients. Sheldon was clear on that. Monroe would not be able to practice medicine without a license. To get around this, they would use Becky's term, "speaking in tongues," to describe what Monroe did. Monroe was no more than an intercessor, praying for each person's good health. No cures were promised.

When the fine print was skimmed, but not thoroughly understood, and the barest legalities accounted for, Sheldon's advertising campaign kicked in. A press conference was called and Monroe once again exhibited his skill using yet another group of sick locals. With an informed media and the word-of-mouth wildfire spread by those who had undergone Monroe's toning, the spin started and the crowds arrived, sometimes by the busload.

Monroe was no longer an idiot, at least not in public. He was Miracle Monroe, the hokiest name he had ever heard. He snorted and laughed under the table; his tears had become dried rivers on his face.

"Ka-twee ka-twee ka-twee, bloop bloop bloop!" Brittany was sneaking down the hall. Monroe was surprised that she could make it to his room without getting caught. His sister was filled with an uncontainable energy that burst from her like a bottle rocket. He pulled the blanket aside as she entered.

As Brittany turned to close the door, she peered out into the hall like a sailor looking for a distant land. She whispered, "The coast is clear," to Monroe and quietly shut the door.

Brittany crawled under the table, shoving her brother over to make room. She pulled the blanket back to its position of concealment. They were left in a hazy darkness that soon filled with their warm breath.

"Look what I brought you," Brittany said, as she fished

into the many pockets of her khaki cargo pants. Skittles –
the tropical kind, a Milky Way candy bar, a red packet of
peanuts, and a somewhat squished banana appeared. "I
don't care what Dad says, I'll make sure you get something
to eat."

Monroe hugged his sister and croaked, "Thanks."

"You're welcome, you silly head."

"Where'd you get this stuff, Britt?"

"The banana's from the kitchen. Sorry, I dropped it
when I yanked it off the bunch."

"A bruised banana's better than no banana."

"An' the peanuts are from the zoo. I didn't feel like eating them at the time, so I saved them. You know how Mom
and Dad are. You never know when they're gonna send us
to our rooms without dinner. The peanuts are good insur-
ance."

"When did you go to the zoo?"

"A couple of weeks ago – with Michelle."

"I didn't know that." The corners of Monroe's mouth
drooped and his brow furrowed.

"You were working, as usual." Brittany sighed. "You
don't get to have any fun, do you?"

It was Monroe's turn to sigh. "Nope," he said. He deftly
dropped this line of conversation by continuing with, "So,
where'd the candy come from? Mom's gonna kill us if she
finds out."

"From the librarian. You know, the nice one with the
big, perfect teeth? She smiles a lot and has a twisty bun in
her hair. Her name's kinda funny."

"Araminta?" said Monroe.

"Yeah, that's her."

"She has a funny body sound, too," Monroe added.

"She does? How's it go?"

"That's just it, it doesn't," said Monroe. "I mean, most
of the time, she has no body sound at all. I've never heard
anyone so quiet. Once in a while, though, she makes a deep
"ohm." It's very relaxing. When I was younger and Mom

and Dad let me go to the library, I'd watch how the kids were when they were around her. She could get even the brattiest kids to behave without doing anything special. It was crazy to watch."

"Geez, is that why I feel so calm around her?"

"Yep, Britt. Even though you can't hear it, you're picking up on her body sound," said Monroe. "So, you were telling me about the candy . . . ."

"Well, after story time Monday, Araminta let us each choose two kinds of candy. An' she wasn't stingy, either. She had a big bowl of all sorts of stuff an' it was so hard to decide. We spread it on the floor so we could see everything. I went with the Milky Way and the Skittles, so I could have both chocolate and fruit. I don't know which I like better, but I like to keep my options open," said Brittany.

"Good idea, kiddo," said Monroe. "You wanna share?"

"You go ahead," she replied wistfully. "You need it more than I do. Dad's so stubborn; he'll make you stay here 'til you are nothing more than old bones."

"Don't you worry about me. I'll get out of here before that happens," he said and added, "Really, Britt, you have to share some of this with me or I'll feel like a selfish old dog."

"Okay, but just give me one of each color of the Skittles and a bite of the Milky Way. I don't much care for the banana, 'specially seeing as how it's mushy on the squished bits."

"How about the peanuts?"

"You can keep 'em all to yourself."

"That's generous of you."

"Not generous, really. Michelle and I are going back to the zoo next week an' I'll just get some more."

"Lucky you," said Monroe. He tore open the package of Skittles. Some of the candy scattered on the floor. Brittany quickly retrieved the errant pieces, sorting out one of each color and giving the duplicates back to Monroe. She savored each Skittle, eating them in a pattern from lightest to darkest.

Monroe tossed a handful into his mouth and allowed the

colors and sounds to meld before swallowing. Then he said, "Okay, Britt, you'd better get out of here before you get in trouble."

"My trouble won't be anything like your trouble."

"Yeah, but just the same . . . ."

"Alright, I'm going," said Brittany as she slipped out from under the table. "You know, Monroe, I can handle anything Mom and Dad dish out."

"You keep talkin' tough, but be quiet when you leave. Make sure you shut the door."

"Got it, Chief!" Brittany saluted and was gone, blooping down the hall.

Monroe leaned against the wall. Soon, his head tipped and he nodded off. Pictures of those who'd come to his healing sessions flashed and faded behind his eyes, blending into one another in a long, disjointed dream. There was a man with chocolaty skin, scarce white hair, and dark, evasive eyes. He sounded like aluminum cans shifting in a black plastic trash bag. A faint bitterness lodged deep in the man, impossible to remove, remove, remove . . . . "What was I saying?" The white-haired man became a white-haired woman, stooped and forgetful, pale blue eyes, milky and confused. Swiss cheese interruptions in her body sound. Thoughts twisting, trying to avoid the holes, but falling . . . falling . . . falling in. Monroe shook his head in his sleep. Can't sew the holes together. Can't do it.

"Help me, help me, please." A child begging, not more than four. Wisps of hair like the chocolate man, but patchy and shorn. Eyes limpid, navy spheres, clearly carrying the weight of the world. Wheezing, gasping, breath not filling her lungs. Air sacs deflated, rigid, smoky and blackened. Deteriorating. Too far gone. Can't help. Tears don't come to the huge eyes overtaking a too small head. These eyes have been disappointed too often to hope. Mother, crying, replaces the oxygen mask and pushes the child away in her wheelchair. Father, stoic, pulls the oxygen tank behind on a small, wheeled cart. In a husky, smoker's voice, he says, "I

told you it was no use coming, no use coming, no use, no use
. . . ."

Shifting, thoughts twisting around Swiss cheese holes.
"No use, Monroe, no use. You're no use to me, Monroe.
You're an idiot, Monroe." Slicka, slicka, slicka. "Let's count
the money. Looks like we made a good haul today. Poor,
sick bastards." Slicka, slicka, slicka. "Monroe, The Miracle
Idiot. Praise be to God!" The sound of lips kissing money
pounded Monroe's ear drums, the membranes pulsating
faster and harder, faster and harder, heart thumping, ear
drums threatening to explode, heart thumping faster and
harder, faster and harder, waking Monroe.

As consciousness intruded, he sat up suddenly and
knocked his head on the table. "Ow! God! Ow! Damn! Ow,
ow, ow!" Monroe cursed and rubbed the sore spot like regular mortals, unable to use his special ability upon himself.

He heard Cricket spinning and flapping a hurricane
dance in his cage, punctuating the motion with loud
squawks. Monroe emerged from under the table, still
massaging his head, and went over to the bird. "It's okay,
Cricket," he said softly, and he whistled and twittered until
the parakeet came to rest upon a perch. Then he opened
the cage door and extended a forefinger to the bird, who
hopped aboard. Monroe carefully maneuvered his passenger through the opening in the bars. He smoothed the green
and yellow feathers of his friend, thinking how easy it would
be to crush Cricket's delicate body. The bird flew from his
finger to a curtain rod, and Monroe was glad for its freedom,
limited though it was by the four walls of his room. Why
did he have to keep this creature caged? It didn't feel right,
but he loved the bird and wanted to guard it, protect it from
the harm it would surely face if released. So little was needed to restrain the bird; the bars of its cage laughably thin and
easy to break for a more powerful being. Monroe watched
as Cricket glided from the curtain rod down to the table,
pulling up short on the oooma lama blanket, strutting and
stretching and burbling pleasantries to himself. A morsel of

freedom was all it took for Cricket to taste happiness.

Unexpectedly, Monroe was engulfed in a pair of arms and a greeting. "Hi, Monroe! How ya doin'?" Distracted by his ruminations, Monroe had shut his ears to sounds outside his room and missed Jenna's approach. He'd been practicing the skill of not listening, but had never been completely successful at it until this moment. Unused to being startled, he jumped.

"Jenna! What are you doing here?"

"What do you mean, what am I doing here?" Jenna mussed Monroe's hair. "Your name is all over the news. Rumors are flying. People think you've been kidnapped."

"No way!"

"Way!" said Jenna. "Mom called and told me you were under the table, refusing to come out. I can't figure out why Dad and Sheldon haven't had a press conference yet to let everyone know you're okay."

"You know Dad. He's milking this for all it's worth," said Monroe, shaking his head. He went over to the bed and sat.

Jenna followed and took a seat beside him. Picking up on his rue, she said, "Is that why you're hiding out?"

"Yeah. Partly. I can't do anything right by him. No matter how much money I earn, it's never enough. I think he hates me."

"Dad doesn't hate you. He just doesn't understand you," said Jenna.

"Nope. He hates me. Why else would he make me sit in church all the time and not give me a chance to do what I want to do?"

"You've got a point there, Monroe. I always thought the healing sessions were excessive. I couldn't figure out how you could do it for so long and not go crazy. You always seemed so cheerful about it."

"Well, I'm not cheerful," Monroe's voice quavered.

"Hey, bud, don't cry," said Jenna as she patted his shoulder. "Have you tried talking to Dad about this?"

"He won't listen."

"That may be, but your only other option is to stay in this room."

"Sounds like a good idea to me. Brittany said she'd bring me food."

"Monroe," Jenna said, "You're going to have to face Dad sometime, pig-headed though he can be." She waited for a response from Monroe. With none forthcoming, she continued, "If you want, I can be there when you talk to him."

"Can't you just tell him how I feel?"

"No. You've got to learn to stick up for yourself."

"It's too hard. You've always defended me and now you're backing out," said Monroe sullenly.

"I'm not backing out. I said I'd be there when you talk to Dad, but now it's your turn to buck up and speak your mind. This will be good practice for when you get out on your own and there's no one else around to take care of you."

Monroe yawned in a fit of nervousness. He'd been holding his breath at the thought of approaching his dad and his body craved and automatically sought extra oxygen. He sighed for good measure and said, "Okay, Jenna, I'll do it. But what do I say?"

"What do you want? Think about that first. Do you want to cut back on the healing sessions?"

"I wouldn't mind stopping altogether," said Monroe.

"I'm not sure Dad's going to be ready for that big a change, but if it's what you want . . . ."

"Yeah, it's what I want," said Monroe. He hesitated and furrowed his brow, concentrating.

Jenna said, "What else?"

"It's just that, well, I'm not sure how to say it . . . ."

"Not sure? Or afraid?"

"Afraid," and he blurted, "I think I'm losing my powers," before he had a chance to stop himself.

At this revelation, several emotions drifted across Jenna's face – surprise, concern, a question mark look – in rapid succession. She settled on calm, but serious, like a sky gray

with high, non-threatening clouds. Monroe caught a stutter-
ing in her body sound, "Ta, ta, ta, ta," skipping the "te" and
landing on "toe, toe, toe." She asked, "How do you know?"
in a gentle, fact-finding tone, allowing no worry to creep into
her expression.

Monroe got up and walked over to the table, where
Cricket had been preening. He bent to the bird's eye level
and addressed it rather than his sister. "In the past few
months I've noticed that I can't seem to pick up on people's
body sounds as easily as I could before. When I do, the
harmony I need to fix them doesn't come through clearly
enough. I'm having to fake sounds and pray they will work,
but I know they're not right. People are going away sick,
even those with diseases I used to be able to cure. I feel
horrible. These people are depending on me and I'm failing
them."

"That's pretty heavy. Any idea why this is happening
now?" Jenna asked.

"I've tried and tried to figure it out. Maybe it's because
I'm working too many hours and I'm tired. I've also been
teaching myself how to close out sounds, but maybe I'm getting too good at it," he said, and gave up with, "Oh, I don't
know."

"Hmm. Those could be contributing factors. Has anything unusual happened to you lately? Have you had the flu
or a cold or something?"

"No. I've been pretty healthy, considering."

"Bumped your head recently? I've heard of people who
develop special powers after hitting their heads. Only with
you, it'd be the reverse."

"Really?"

"Yeah, but it's generally a pretty hard hit, like, enough to
knock you out or give you a concussion."

"I guess me bumping my head under the table is out
then." Monroe laughed and rubbed his tender spot.

"You're right," Jenna said, "That probably wouldn't do
it." She reclined on the bed, legs dangling over the side,

and stared in contemplation at the ceiling. Monroe waited, watching her. He could hear her body sound slip into concentration mode, slowing down and hiccupping periodically as she turned thoughts around in her mind. Something clicked inside and she sat up. "How old are you? Wait a minute, dumb question. Sixteen, right?"

"Yeah. What's that got to do with anything?"

"You're a teenager, dopey. All kinds of strange things happen to kids in puberty. Big feet, big noses, acne, sleeping all the time, hormones raging . . . ."

"Voices cracking?"

"Exactly. Maybe, just maybe, this is your unique way of going through puberty."

"Losing my hearing and my healing powers?" Monroe looked a little disappointed at the thought.

"Don't be glum, Monroe. Puberty is your way out, your ticket to the land of mere mortals. You can stop listening to people, like the rest of us, and not have to be responsible for healing everyone who happens along."

"When you put it that way . . . ."

"Sorry, Monroe, I didn't mean to be flippant. This is big for you, especially if the changes are permanent. It'll take some getting used to, but at least you have an out with Dad. If the changes are a real physical process for you, he can't deny them."

"That's true," said Monroe, "If I don't have my powers, I can have a normal life, can't I?" As he spoke, he got Cricket to hop from the oooma lama blanket onto his finger and took the bird back to its cage. He permitted a puff of relief to escape his lips as he considered the promise of his eventual freedom.

"As normal as normal can be, but you have to tell him first." Jenna said.

Monroe's desperation returned. "What if Dad doesn't believe me? What if he makes me keep doing the healings even if they're no longer working? What if he gets mad? He'll yell at me and I hate it when he yells at me."

"Hurts, doesn't it?"

"You have no idea. My eardrums feel like they're going to explode."

"God, Monroe, I never thought of that, how it would affect your hearing. I was just thinking about how much his yelling gets to me emotionally."

"The damage isn't just emotional, Jenna. It can make you physically sick, like being doused in caustic chemicals."

"Wow, really? I can see why you're afraid to talk to him."

"Please, please, please . . . can you do it?" Monroe whined.

"No, Monroe. This is your life. You've got to come clean with him, even if he yells. I'll back you up, if it gets too intense, and you'll get through it," said Jenna. "The bigger problem will be if he insists that you fake healings. If he does that, I'll find a way to get you out of here. You can come stay with me."

"Are you sure?"

"Sure, I'm sure. A big sister's gotta take care of her brother, doesn't she?" Jenna rose from the bed, squeezed Monroe's forearm and said, "Now, think about what you want to say, take a deep breath, and let's go talk to Dad before you chicken out."

Story 4

Miss Fortune

Her fingers fumbled over the alarm's keypad. She was late for a reading. One of the library patrons, a nosy, gruff old guy who had nothing better to do, kept her late looking up automobile values. It didn't do to just hand him the N.A.D.A. guide. He couldn't read the tiny print or figure out the value deduction for mileage. It was easier to do it herself, which he preferred. He was lonely and she was company. Normally, she was more understanding – after all, she was married to the man in another life – but, not today, not when she was late and trying to set a tricky alarm with the door key in hand and two heavy book bags and a purse swinging from her arms. If she didn't turn this thing on correctly, an alarm would be sent to the police station and that minor complication would leave her client waiting on her doorstep past the point of decency. While her clients accepted a certain flakiness, they wouldn't put up with lateness. It was unprofessional.

"There, it's set," she said, and she hurried through the heavy door, her bags banging against her thighs as she turned to lock it. She hustled to her lime green VW in the parking lot, clicking her remote so it would be unlocked when she reached it. She flung the book bags onto the back seat. Their contents spilled onto the floor.

"Shit!"

No time to deal with that now. She had to change,

transform herself to meet her client's expectations. Her usual outfit was at home, and if Harvey hadn't delayed her, this wouldn't be a problem. She'd have to make do. She removed the bobby pins holding her braided bun in place as she glanced through the car hoping to find something, anything, that would work. There, on the front passenger seat, crushed underneath a pile of books and a CD case, was her translucent purple shawl with glittering metallic threads. Perfect, except for the wrinkles. She unbuttoned the top two buttons of her white satin blouse and untucked it from her skirt. Thankfully, she had worn the gray broomstick skirt. It gave her credibility. She pulled the shawl from beneath the detritus on the seat, shook it out, threw it over her shoulders and tied the loose ends to keep it in place.

She yanked off the pony-holder at the bottom of her braid as she jumped into the driver's seat and started the engine. While she drove, she undid the braid and combed through her waist-length, coal-dark hair with her fingers. Its kinky unkemptness provided the right look.

Maneuvering the VW through Greenville's west side, she headed to Green Street to cross the river bridge. A simple right turn onto this main thoroughfare took forever because of rush-hour traffic. Her fingers tapped the steering wheel, willing a break between cars. Once she got into the traffic stream, the signal lights in the old section on the east side of town stalled the flow of cars on the bridge. She muttered a few choice words and then stopped herself. This was not the proper mood for a reading. Instead, she imagined positive energy pooling around her and rummaged through the glove box, finding a dozen thin silver bracelets and a pair of dangly earrings with rose quartz stones to add to her outfit. She was congratulating herself for her habit of leaving stuff in the VW when a car horn honked behind her. A massive, black SUV was bearing down on her, filling her rearview mirror.

"Hold your horses! I'm going, I'm going," she yelled. Even though the windows were up and the driver couldn't

hear her, she knew he'd feel her irritation and take it out
on his family when he got home. That's the way the world
worked. Energy followed intention. And her intention,
what with her tardiness, was less than charitable. What did
it mean, getting upset at such a silly circumstance? She'd
have to figure that out later. She turned north on Thirteenth
Avenue, east on Red Street, and finally pulled her car into
her driveway.

There was her client, on the stoop, attempting to look
through the skinny windows on either side of her door. Of
course, he couldn't see through them; they had curtains.
She had put them up just last week. For years now her
clients kept peeking into her house, trying to get a read on
her. They wanted to see how a witch lived – that's what
they thought she was; a witch. The laugh was on them. She
was an atheist, not a Wiccan. The voyeurism had recently
begun to get on her nerves, but she could hardly blame her
clients. She had encouraged their erroneous beliefs, partially
because the acting was a thrill, mostly because they really
wanted her to be a witch. While she was tired of their curi-
osity and superstition, she acquiesced a bit with the curtain
fabric; a black velveteen to which she had affixed gold lamé
stars and moons. *Let the illusion continue*, she thought as she
grabbed her purse, adjusted her shawl, and got out of the
car.

The man, who had heard her drive up and turned to
face her, was standing with arms crossed, foot tapping and
brow furrowed. He was delicate in build, not much over
five feet, but his attitude was much bigger than his posture
or size would suggest. She felt his energy pushing against
her as she walked up the sidewalk. She took a full breath for
strength and subconsciously threaded her car key between
her index and middle fingers.

As she reached the steps and ascended, he said, "You're
late," in a low snarl and poked his watch face to punctuate
the statement.

"It's a pleasure to meet you, too, Mr. Gibson." She shifted the keys into her left hand and stuck out her right hand in order to force him to shake it. "I'm Miss Fortune, but you may call me Araminta." She pumped his arm, squeezing his long, fine fingers. She could break them if she had to. It was best to meet a bully with unwavering fortitude.

He backed down a bit, his eyes softening. "Sorry . . . Mom would be appalled by my manners . . . nice to meet you . . . I prefer Hugo."

The words came out in a rush, air mixed into the syllables, dulling the previous harshness. This was the voice she recognized from his phone call. She had sensed a rift in Hugo's personality when he had made the appointment, but she liked to reserve judgment on clients until she could meet them. This breathiness was a disguise, an attempt to get his voice to match his physique. His real voice was the "You're late" one; deep, like a cannon booming in a cave – more appropriate to a towering, bulky-chested guy. Instead, Hugo looked soft and precious, with downy hair the color of dry winter wheat that curled and retreated from his forehead. His eyes were pale, watery. His sharpest feature was his nose, pointy and well-pressed, like his clothing. *Me-ti-cu-lous*, thought Araminta.

He stood firm on the top step, not allowing Araminta to get to the door. "You're still late, you know," he said.

"And getting later by the moment, Mr., er, Hugo." He was being obstinate, but Araminta didn't feel malice in his intent. If she had, she would've jabbed him with her keys and run. No, he was just trying to prove a point, much to her annoyance. "If you wouldn't mind . . . ." She advanced to push past him. He got the hint and moved aside.

"Excuse me, sorry," he said as she opened the door.

"Come in."

"Shouldn't I remove my shoes?"

"No need." Araminta headed to the kitchen to heat water for tea. "Would you like something to drink? I've got spritzers, cranberry juice, water or tea," she called out to him.

"Really, I can take them off."

"Don't bother. I'm not particular and the floors can take it." She waited for him to respond to her question or join her in the kitchen. A couple of beats and a pause later, she stuck her head out the kitchen door and looked down the hall.

Hugo hung at the front entry. He was raking his hand through his hair and looking at his shoes. Araminta almost laughed at him. He was obviously struggling between his desire for neatness and a need to follow her orders.

"Look, suit yourself, Hugo. If you're more comfortable without shoes, take them off . . . no biggy."

"Okay." He looked relieved.

"Drink?" she reminded him.

"Uh, yeah, what're you having?"

"Tea."

"I'll have some of that."

"Alright. Why don't you make yourself comfortable in here?" She led him to the reading room. A curtain matching those in the front entry windows hung in the doorway. (She'd been quite industrious last week.) She pulled it aside. He stepped into the dim room and stalled, letting his eyes adjust to the light.

Araminta entered behind him and said, "A little dark, isn't it? I'll light some candles." She plucked an electric candle lighter off a bookshelf near the door and bustled about the room, setting wicks aflame. When she was finished, the thirty-odd candles threw a wavering full-moon glow about the room. "There. That's better. Have a seat and I'll be back in a minute with the tea."

Araminta took her time freshening up in the bathroom. She fussed with preparing the tea service in the kitchen. The timing was critical. She wanted her clients to become familiar with the reading room, start poking around the floor-to-ceiling bookshelf on the east wall, notice her spoon collection, try the cushy armchairs in the corners. The candlelight would freak them out a little and they'd push back layers of gauzy drapes over the windows only to find them shuttered

from the outside. A smidgen of claustrophobia was good.
They avoided the round table in the center of the room. This
was all that was left of what had once been a cheery dining
room.

A crystal ball, inherited from her grandmother, sat on
the end of the table furthest from the door. A true crystal
ball, like this one, was smaller than a baseball, not a huge
head-sized fakey one often shown in old movies. It beckoned her clients, urging them to come closer for a look.
Though they tried to resist out of respect for their hostess
– Lord knew what a witch could do if you messed with
her things – inevitably they'd gaze into it. The candlelight
flickered within, drawing them into a trance, leaving their
brains foggy and disconnected from reality. This was what
she wanted.

She waited and listened and when she felt the time was
right, she carried the tea tray into the room.

"What kept you?" Hugo said, the hardness back in his
voice. He wasn't foggy or disoriented in the least and he was
sitting in her chair, the one nearest the crystal ball, the one
that put her in the best possible feng shui position, facing
the door. Her other clients stood to look in the crystal ball.
Intuitively, they felt they shouldn't sit in her chair. What was
up with this guy?

"What kept me?" She placed the tray on a side table.
"Just getting the tea. What kind would you like? I have
several varieties. Why don't you come over and pick some
out?"

Hugo stayed put and said, "Not just now. I mean, what
held you up before? Why were you late?"

Jesus, did he ever quit? She faced him, squared her
shoulders and said, "That, sir, is none of your business."

"When it comes to my appointments, it becomes my
business."

Her veins prickled, the ice forming in them crackling off
her tongue. "The only time of mine that is your business is
that which is scheduled for a reading. Nothing more. I'm

sorry I was late, but if you don't drop this immediately, I will cancel this appointment."

Hugo put his hands up and lowered his eyes in submission. "Consider it dropped." The airiness returned to his voice.

"Why don't you come get some tea and we'll get started."

Hugo got out of her chair. Inwardly she sighed in relief. He picked ginger, a tea that, while good for abdominal ailments, could burn a delicate stomach - obviously not his problem. Feeling a bit dyspeptic herself, she chose peppermint. She was hoping it would relax her.

"Help yourself to honey or sugar."

"Sure, thanks." Hugo sunk five sugar cubes into his mug, taking care to pick up each with the mini tongs. When he dropped one on the floor, he slyly nudged it under the table, cast her a sidelong glance, and added five more cubes as though nothing untoward had happened. Araminta played along, pretending not to notice, hoping the ants who called her kitchen home wouldn't get to it before she did, and offered Hugo a spoon from among several she had in a small basket on the tea tray. As a spoon collector, she liked to keep a variety of decorative spoons available for guests and clients. It was her little Rorschach test, with the style of the preferred spoon dishing up a bite-sized personality profile. Hugo picked a plain spoon, the most austere of the lot. Form follows function. *That, or the guy is tight-fisted and I'll have a helluva time getting paid*, she thought.

She preferred ornate spoons, her souvenir spoon collection containing primarily filigree and plique-à-jour spoons. The latter, which looked as though they were mini stained glass windows, were her favorite, but darned hard to come by. She had recently begun collecting animal spoons. She had two in her skirt pocket at the moment; one with an alligator handle and a bowl with a picture of Seminole Indians canoeing on the Miami River, the other, which commemorated the 1905 Lewis and Clark expedition exposition, had a dapper frog for a handle.

As Hugo prepared his tea, she was trying to decide which of these she would use during the reading. The alligator had a fearsome expression, with its forced toothy smile and wrinkly neck. It would give her strength. The dapper frog, dressed in its finest suit and accessorized with a quirky grin, made her smile. She could use some levity with this client. The spoon she chose would not stir her tea. As souvenir spoons, they weren't meant for that. The tea gave the spoon a reason to be on her table; the spoon had a higher purpose. During a reading, she needed something concrete to focus on in the present, something that would bring her back when it was time.

The crystal ball had been her grandmother's focusing agent, and as such, it didn't work for Araminta. She kept it as a prop, establishing a moody ambiance for her clients. No one would ever take her seriously if she admitted that she did spoon readings, although that wasn't what she was do-ing, just like Grandma Clotilda didn't really read the crystal ball. People were apt to make inane assumptions, so if she had placed the spoon in front of her during a reading, they would naturally think she was picking up images on it as though it were a hand-held DVD player or something. Nor would clients believe her if she claimed that she could con-duct readings in broad daylight, rather than in a darkened room. They were so silly with their cravings for drama. If they could let go of the theatrics, they wouldn't need her for insight on their problems.

After the tea was poured, Araminta took her place at the table and directed Hugo to the chair opposite. Chance picked her spoon; the alligator won. This she placed just be-hind the crystal ball, where she could look at it while giving the illusion of ball gazing. She closed her eyes and breathed deeply. She opened her eyes and saw Hugo wearing an imperious expression, a glare sliding precisely down his nose, like an archer's arrow let fly.

One more breath quelled a niggling unease and

allowed her to concentrate on Hugo's essence, rather than
his brusqueness. As she entered a trance state, she idled in
neutral as a piece of her soul slipped out of her body. This
out-of body experience was the same as those reported by
others, what with the silver cord and a portion of the soul
left behind in order to protect the physical being, except
that Araminta had inherited the ability to bring it on at will.
Her sisters, Odile and Adrienne, could do the same, but had
decided to remain in the real world, rather than trot around
in the Soul-o-sphere. Truth be told, Araminta didn't care
for the spiritual implications of the word 'soul,' but it was
good shorthand until science could dissect and explain this
ephemeral consciousness that gave human beings their vital-
ity.

Her soul, disconnected from the sluggish material realm,
hovered around Hugo, directly reading his energy, his life's
intent. If she'd had to describe what she was sensing, she'd
say that she had unhinged herself from the space/time con-
tinuum, to a place of no time and no space, but that wasn't
it exactly, because if she was some place, she was occupying
space. No, this realm was more all space/all time.

Hugo's past and future lives were arrayed for Araminta's
perusal, but she wasn't interested in all of them, just the
ones that, through unresolved conflicts, were impeding his
current life. One stuck out, a brass thread in a tapestry of
muted greens and browns. The man before her had led
hundreds of safe and orderly lives, lock-stepping with the
lowliest, not daring to distinguish himself, except for this
one. Her soul zoomed from the macrocosmic view into the
microcosm of Hugo's notable life thread. As she entered his
past life, she transmitted what she was experiencing back to
the portion of soul left with her body via the silver cord.

"Hugo Gibson? Are you with me?" The pitch of
Araminta's voice lowered, the words wavering across her
tongue. This was not done for effect, but resulted from her
split soul.

Hugo rolled his eyes and leaned back in his chair.

"Yeah, haven't left my seat, in case you haven't noticed."

"I'm on a battlefield . . . not sure where, yet . . . let me get my bearings."

"You can quit trying. I've never been in combat . . . ."

"The uniforms are not current or American . . . hold on . . . I think I'm in Africa."

"Are you crazy? What kind of peanut gallery are you running here?"

"This is one of your past lives, one that has great bearing on your life right now. Yes, this is Africa, in an area that is now part of the country of South Africa."

"Past lives? What a load of crap. You expect me to pay you for this?"

"It's 1901."

"That's it. I'm not taking any more of this bullshit." Hugo stood so abruptly that he about knocked his chair over backwards. He caught it and shoved it at the table, causing tremors in the tea and the alligator spoon. He made for the curtained doorway, but stopped as Araminta continued her reading.

"You're a British officer. I'm not sure how I know this. You have no rank markings on your uniform and . . . this is weird . . . the buttons on your uniform . . . they're painted out. They match your uniform. Ahh . . . yes, I see now . . . they . . . the buttons and the uniform . . . blend with the veld."

Hugo stalled between the door and his chair. "The veld? What's that?"

"The countryside. Rough land here. Scrubby, dirty, dry. There are *kopjes* – hills. There are rivers, filthy, rough rivers when they are flowing, gullies when they're not. This is a tough place to live, a tough place to fight."

"You say I'm an officer?"

"Yes. That is clear. You carry yourself as a leader, an officer. I see that you have a gun . . . a rifle, well cleaned, with a shiny bayonet."

His interest fully piqued, Hugo returned to his seat. "Go

on," he said.

"I'm smaller than you are; my skin is dark, but not black .... I'm not a native of Africa." This was strange. Normally during a reading, Araminta's soul floated outside the main action, watching everything in a third-person sort of way. Somehow, her soul had hitched itself to a small, bony dark man. "Yes . . . that's it . . . I'm from India and I'm bearing stretchers for the British in this war . . . my friend, who is native, is helping me."

Hugo's foot tapped under the table. "I don't want to hear about you. What about me? The British officer. Tell me about that."

"I'm getting to it . . . give me a minute . . . there's more here than the war. You have power, but not just the power associated with being an officer. Everyone listens to your commands without hesitation . . . ."

"Naturally," Hugo said. A smirk settled on his face. He rested his chin in his palms as he braced himself on the table with his elbows. *That's the way it should be*, he thought. *Everyone listening to me, doing what I say without hesitation. Jumping when I say jump.*

"They're afraid of you, too."

"As they should be."

"My friend and I, we don't like your gun . . . or the bayonet, which we often see you sharpening. It is like a razor, the sun glinting prettily off it . . . so sharp that a man would not even feel its mortal cut, but would only realize his wound upon the sight of his unstemmable blood."

"The only useful knife is a sharp knife. It must be so sharp that it will slice through bone like a ripe tomato," Hugo said. Araminta's body shuddered imperceptibly.

"Things are becoming clearer . . . . The British are fighting the Boers, farmers of Dutch descent, trying to establish the dominant government . . . trying to control lands of diamonds and gold."

"What year did you say it was?"

"1901."

"My God. You're talking about the second Boer War. I was a British officer in the Boer War?"

"It appears that is the case. But there's something else here . . . something to do with diamonds."

With this, Hugo's pale eyes hardened and twinkled like the precious faceted stone, anticipating the intrigue he felt in Araminta's tone. "Diamonds, yes? Do continue."

"Inyanga, my friend, is in your tent." Araminta paused momentarily. She recognized Inyanga as someone in her current life – her best friend Maureen. This she kept to herself as she went on. "It is late, darkest night. He has no business being in your tent, not as a stretcher bearer, not at this time of day. I see him coming out of your tent and catch up to him. When we are out of earshot, he shows me what you have given him. He has received a folded bit of fabric from you. It is filled with diamonds. Uncut diamonds. You have asked Inyanga to give the diamonds to a man the next day, a man who will pretend to be wounded in battle, but will smuggle the diamonds out of the country after his time in the field hospital."

"A good plan. What use do the natives have for diamonds? All these riches under their feet, diamonds, gold, platinum, silver, and they can't figure out how to use them, to leverage them to create a wealthy country. No, they dance and sing and lead puny, insignificant lives instead." Hugo snorted in derision. "Still, they aren't as bad as those bloody Boers, who are so uncivilized that they can't stop fighting with each other. Don't know how to rule a country, either. We British, we know what we are doing, know how countries should be run. That's why we have colonies all over the world, to show the ignorant how to govern. To rule people who can't rule themselves." His voice had reached cannon level again, shaking the soul that remained with Araminta's body. He was reliving the mental aspects of the past life as though his present life were mere skin on the surface of milk, a thin, easily skimmable veneer.

This wasn't the way it was supposed to work. Her readings generally produced déjà vu in her clients, not an all-out reliving of a past life. Araminta wanted to return, end this now. She gulped the warm air of the reading room, candle vapor mingling among her teeth and wafting into her nasal cavity through the back of her throat. Her eyes settled on the alligator spoon. Comforted and strengthened by the spoon, she held on, knowing this reading was as much about her as it was him.

"I told Inyanga that this was not right, this smuggling business. He'd get hurt for sure. Inyanga said that you'd offered him money, a month's wages as stretcher carrier, to do this thing for him. This would be the only time. You promised him. The money would help feed his children, who were in one of the camps, their flesh melting from their bones. You'd personally arrange for them to be fed. You promised this, knowing that your promise was a false one. Inyanga knew this, but was frightened. If he didn't do as you asked, you'd kill him, and then who would take care of his children?"

"His bloody children, that's all he talks about. He and his children aren't worth the scrub and stones beneath my feet," Hugo said.

"But, you promised."

"Who keeps promises? He's a foolish man to believe in them," said Hugo.

"It is a foolish man who makes a promise he does not intend to keep."

"How dare you speak to me that way, Onkar!"

Araminta felt her soul skip like the tip of a needle hastily placed on a vinyl record album. How did he know her Indian name? It was as though he were doing the reading, not she. The silver cord connecting her life as Onkar, the stretcher bearer, to her life as Araminta, the fortune-teller and librarian, was trembling, as was her physical being in both lives.

Onkar bowed, repentant. "Sorry, sir. Forgive me, sir. I do not know my place, sir."

"Don't get out of line again. If ever you are tempted, just remember what happened to Khonsa."

Onkar shuddered at the mention of Khonsa's name. Khonsa had been a kind man, so gentle, but sad. He was separated from his beloved, to whom he was betrothed; their wedding a suspended promise awaiting the day when Khonsa would be done serving as a guide, showing the British soldiers the way over the veld. Khonsa had introduced Inyanga to Onkar. Through Inyanga, Onkar learned that Khonsa's intended was ill. This made him sadder and more desperate to be with her. Khonsa was the first to be taken into the diamond smuggling plot, having been promised a leave to tend his ailing fiancé. When he changed his mind and tried to back out of his role as mule, this man, a British officer then, Hugo Gibson now, had gleefully stabbed him with his bayonet in view of Inyanga. Hugo then ordered Inyanga to get rid of the body.

"No, sir . . . stay in line, I will, sir." As Onkar groveled, Araminta fought to maintain control of the reading. "Khonsa . . . he is the man you call Tin in your life as Hugo Gibson."

"The Tin Man? You've got to be kidding," said Hugo.

"No, sir."

"What a loser. A pathetic excuse of a man. Panhandling, sucking off the system, trash heap for a house. Living on the flats, he's probably polluting the river."

"He has integrity, sir. He had it as Khonsa, he has it now, sir." Why the hell was she still calling him 'sir'?

"Integrity, schmegrity," Hugo said. "Where does that get you in life? I'll tell you where. Dead, that's where. Buried in the ground, fucking worm food, completely forgotten."

"Integrity is never forgotten in the universe."

"What do you know?" said Hugo.

It was no good arguing. Trying to prove a point would take too much energy away from this reading, and Araminta had precious little of that to spare. Hugo would have to

learn the hard way, dedicating many more lives to the les-
sons of integrity, how integrity practiced in human beings
rippled through all of creation, relieving humanity of much
suffering. Still, Araminta was angry at this hard-bitten,
crass and cruel man sitting before her. So angry that she
was prepared to snap back into her body and throttle him.
She told herself to get a grip, looked at the leering alligator
spoon with the peacefully rowing Seminoles, and continued
scanning Hugo's life as a British officer.

"I'm jumping ahead a bit in your past life," she said.
"Let's see . . . your diamond smuggling operation is running
smoothly. Inyanga has moved several packets for you . . .
and . . . oh my God!"

"What? What's happening?" asked Hugo. "Oh, wait a
minute. Let me guess. I killed Inyanga, didn't I? Skewered
him with my beautiful bayonet. Bloody sop deserved it, just
like Khonsa."

"You bastard! How could you?" Araminta's heart skittered and thumped, trying to escape her chest cavity. "All he
wanted was to take care of his children," she sobbed.

"It's no matter. They'll die in the camps soon enough,
what with all the typhoid and dysentery going around."

"You're the most heartless man I've ever met," said
Araminta.

"At least I'm not late to my appointments." Hugo leaned
on the table and sneered at her.

Araminta felt her root chakra go cold as fear flooded the
silver cord from both ends of her connected lives. *Damn!
How did he know where this was going? But he couldn't know
completely, or he wouldn't be here for a reading. Okay, Araminta,
baby, time to get control of this situation.* She steadied her emotions and extricated herself from her life as Onkar, which
was feeding her fear. She scanned fore and aft along both of
Hugo's lives in order to regain the calm of prescience. She
knew that every life possibility, every choice along a person's time line was open and available, but that people were
achingly predictable. Once they chose a course of action,

rarely did they do a complete about-face. Hugo, with his tidy nature, was going to do just what she expected of him. Her prophetic scan complete, she continued in a level tone, "I was next, wasn't I, Hugo?"

"Yes."

"Your next diamond mule. I hope you realize that I didn't want to do it."

"It's more fun to force those who resist. Besides, you knew what was going on, knew what had happened to Khonsa and Inyanga. I had to find a way to keep you from talking. Not that anyone would listen to you, a mere Indian, but I couldn't take any chances. I had a good thing going, a very good thing."

"Good for your pockets, rotten for your soul," replied Araminta.

"As you can see by the fact that I'm sitting before you, I didn't spend any time roasting in the fires of Hell. Look, not even a singed eyebrow."

"The fires of Hell aren't literal, but figurative. Your childhood in this life wasn't a good one, was it?"

"What's that got to do with anything?"

"Plenty. Though you shed the bodies of your lives through death, your soul continues on," said Araminta.

"I still don't see what my life as a British officer in the Boer War has to do with my childhood, which was fine, by the way."

"Deny it all you want, but your childhood was less than ideal. Your father, he came and went continually. You didn't know when to expect him. Your mother, she was nasty, abusive, wasn't she?" Araminta was goading him, treading dangerous waters.

"How dare you say such a thing!" Hugo picked up the edge of the table and slammed it down on the floor, upsetting the teacups and jarring the alligator spoon from its spot. Araminta instinctively grabbed the crystal ball to keep it from tipping.

"Knocked you around good, didn't she? Left ugly

purple bruises with her thick, squat hands. No matter how hard you tried to anticipate it, you never saw her attacks coming," Araminta said, verbally holding her own as Hugo lurched around to her side of the table.

His hands, with their long, delicate fingers, were wrapped around her neck, squeezing her larynx from behind. Onkar was suffering the same treatment. Araminta saw Onkar's silver cord start to slip away from his life. If she wasn't careful, hers would, too, and, while she knew that she would simply move on to another life, this wasn't her time. She relaxed into the chokehold, feigning physical collapse. Her grandmother called it playing possum. Strict breath control and muscle relaxation could trick an attacker into backing off. The procedure suited Grandma Clotilda's non-violent nature, though Araminta's exuberant personality had prevented her from seeing its benefit until now. It seemed to be working. Hugo's grip loosened . . . and then tightened again, unrelentingly constricting her throat. Araminta made a mantra of the word "relax" and concentrated on slowing her breathing. Reee-lax, in, out, reee-lax, in, out, reee-lax, in . . . .

And then he did it. He opened his jagged, vile mouth and said the one thing that made her want to fight back, instead of playing possum.

"You lazy, good-for-nothing . . . . You were late. I was waiting for your delivery and you were late. That is unacceptable! Why were you late, Onkar? If it wasn't for you, I'd still be alive."

"You egotistical S.O.B." Araminta was seized with a rage that her grandmother had attempted to cultivate out of her. She reached into her skirt pocket and pulled out her spoon. It was the dapper frog who was destined to rescue her. She leapt up from her slump, startling Hugo with her suddenness, and stabbed him between the eyes with the frog's top hat. He doubled over and dropped to his knees.

"I was not the reason for your death. If you would've given me half a chance to speak, instead of ranting on about

my lateness and choking me into silence, I would've told
you that Boer commandos were in the vicinity and ready
to strike. But would you listen? No." She gave him a kick
to the head before he could recover and go for her again.
"While I was on the ground trying to catch my breath, you
decided you had to get rid of me permanently, didn't you
Cecil? You were too goddamn busy affixing your bayonet to
hear the hoof beats. Isn't that right, Cecil?"

"Don't call me that!"

"Cecil, Cecil, Cecil! That's your given name, isn't it?"
Araminata threw a few more jabs with the spoon and kicked
him again.

"No! I'm Hugo, not Cecil."

"Cecil, the sissy," Araminta chided, knowing she was
rubbing it in.

Hugo wept and whined, "I'm not a sissy."

"On the contrary. When you served in the Boer War,
your name was Cecil."

"Please, stop saying that name!" Hugo brought his
hands up to his ears.

Araminta thundered, "Listen to me." Cowering, lip
quivering, Hugo uncovered his ears.

Araminta crouched next to Hugo, gently placed a hand
on his wrist, and held his fluid, hurt gaze in a beam of
compassion. "Your parents named you Cecil in this life, too,
didn't they?"

His voice caught as he whispered, "Yes."

"And you changed it to Hugo, because you told yourself
it was more manly."

"Yes." He wanted to look away, but Araminta wouldn't
let him.

"You thought that if you had a strong, masculine name,
you could defend yourself, right?"

He nodded.

"But, it's not about your name. Cecil, Hugo, it doesn't
matter."

"It doesn't?"

"No. What you've got to understand is this . . . . Your parents in this life, they were among the group that attacked your tent that day. Like me, your mother was male in that life. She was the one who shot you."

Baby

The box was barely a box, crumbling as it was from
mildew and mouse chews. The smell of it made her
nose itch. Hard to believe it was once sturdy enough to
carry a TV. It was filled with baby clothes, at least as far as
she could tell. She had only peeked through a few of the
top layers. The donor, a harried woman in her mid-thirties
named Nancy, had brought the box to the museum a couple
of weeks ago, along with some unidentified photos and miscellaneous family papers and geegaws. There was the usual
Greenville centennial plate, a handful of pens from past local
businesses, a military medal, an inscribed gold pocket watch,
and a rusted pre-electricity clothes iron. The museum had
too many of these irons to count, but Maureen had accepted
this one because of the value of the rest of the collection.
Several of the photos showed views of the Donken McGee
sawmill that she had never seen. The medal and pocket
watch were good additions to the general collection, but
it was the baby clothes that most excited Maureen. They
were from the early 1970s, an era not well represented in the
museum's collections. Most people didn't consider items
younger than fifty years old to be historically important, so
the museum was perpetually short of what was known in
the profession as contemporary collections. Maureen was
already imagining the exhibit she could mount that would
contrast these baby clothes with the earlier ones the museum

owned.

Nancy had worn these clothes. The box had been found in her dead mother's barn. That was all Maureen could get out of Nancy when she had accepted the collection. It was critical to capture the provenance of artifacts as soon as they entered the museum because there might not be another chance. People moved, got busy, or died. When they were ready to give precious mementos to a museum, it was the end of the line, for them or the artifacts, and they were ready to wash their hands of the whole business. Maureen had tried to elicit further history about this collection, but Nancy did no more than mumble something about her fuzzy memory and her mother's junk. She abruptly signed the donation form and left without giving any further useful details.

Absolutely no sentimentality in that one, thought Maureen, as she pulled a half a dozen little long-sleeved undershirts out of the box and lined them up on the table to examine them. They were made of white cotton that had yellowed and showed signs of water staining, or maybe old baby spittle. A bit of mold was forming around the cuffs and Maureen noted some rust around the metal front snaps. Museum protocol called for a minimal amount of cleaning of incoming artifacts – excessive cleaning wasn't supposed to be good for them – but Maureen could see that she was going to have to give these undershirts, plus most of the other clothes, a good washing before she packed them away. She didn't want the mold to get out of hand. She placed the undershirts into a plastic grocery bag, so she could take them home at the end of the day, and reached back into the box.

Out came a pair of knitted pink baby booties. Maureen melted into her chair and marveled at the tiny slippers. As she did so, an old desire whomped her square in the stomach. How she had wanted a baby! Because she knew the wish would remain unfulfilled, she had tried to put it behind her. She was mostly successful in the effort, but sometimes the desire tiptoed up to her, tapped her on the shoulder and said, "Remember me?"

She set the booties behind the box, so she couldn't see them, and attempted to blank her mind. If she didn't allow her brain to spiral into recrimination, regret, and rage, she'd be okay. The booties could wait.

Back into the box her hands went. Out came a thermal blanket, ragged on one corner. Maureen pictured a mini Nancy alternately gnawing on the blanket and sucking her thumb for comfort. Maybe she'd be less uptight if she still had her blankie.

The box held other goodies – several pairs of cotton twill pants, one with strawberries and vines crawling over it; long and short-sleeved shirts in a variety of stripes and colors; a furry, red winter jacket; a stack of cloth diapers and rubber pants; and three fancy baby dresses, one pale green with smocking, one pink with a Peter Pan collar, and one white with lavender flowers embroidered on the yoke. Maureen wondered if some of the pants and shirts had come from the Garanimals collection, the once-popular mix-and-match clothing line. Or was that for older children? Judging by their size, these clothes were definitely for infants. A look at the faded labels confirmed that they were for the under-one set.

"Smelly, smelly, you are," Maureen said, "But not that delicious baby smell. Yech!" She added the diapers and rubber pants to the undershirts and thermal blanket already in the to-launder bag and started a new bag for the rest of the clothing. The jacket would have to stay behind until she could figure out how to wash it without ruining the nap.

The remainder of the box contained ten flannel receiving blankets with crocheted borders and a crib-sized quilt. Maureen spread the quilt out on an empty table. She wanted a closer look. The pattern was log cabin, arranged in a barn raising set, with tints of greens and yellows alternating in a diagonal bulls-eye effect. She surmised that whoever made this quilt for Nancy began it before her birth. Green and yellow were the default colors for baby shower gifts when the sex of an infant was unknown.

Maureen examined the stitching. "Goodness! This is hand-pieced!" Maureen had put together a few quilts in her time, but she had always pieced the blocks on a sewing machine, having no patience for hand-sewing them. "Somebody sure loved you, Nancy-girl."

Maureen sighed. It was decision time. She stood by the table with her hands on her hips, eyes glazed in concentration, only vaguely focused on the quilt. To take it home, or not? She vacillated. With the clothing, diapers and receiving blankets, she'd have at least three bags of stuff to wash. She'd have to sort everything by type and color, so she didn't inadvertently wreck something, which meant a lot of little loads and quite a bit of time. A few items were going to have to be hand-washed, including this quilt. It was Saturday; the museum was closed Sundays and Mondays, so she'd have a couple of days to work on the laundry. But, then again, George would want attention, and, if she took the quilt home, she'd be carrying an extra bag. Three, along with her purse, was plenty for the walk. "That's it," she said.

"What's it?"

Maureen was startled out of her reverie by Kate, one of the museum's volunteers. She was carrying a clipboard and pen.

"Jeez, Kate, hi. You're very good at sneaking up and scaring the daylights out of a person."

"And you're fun to scare," said Kate with a smile. "You must've jumped a good three inches. You should've seen the look on your face."

"Ha, ha. How nice of you to laugh at my distress. Are you making the temp and humidity rounds?"

"Yeah, I thought I'd start up here so I could visit you in your attic hidey-hole, Miss Mole."

"Miss Mole? Oh, you are a laugh riot, Miss Smarty Pants."

"I try," said Kate as she bowed her head. "What are you working on?"

"A collection of baby clothes. They were crammed in this box and they reek to high heaven."

"Baby clothes? Can I see?"

"Sure," said Maureen. She put the empty box on the floor, shoving it under the table with her toe, and pulled some of the clothes out of the to-launder bags, spreading them on the table so Kate could have a good look.

"How sweet! These dresses are too pretty for words. Can I pick one up?"

"If you're careful."

"The flowers on this dress are nummy. I don't think I've ever had a dress this beautiful," said Kate.

"If you think that's nice, check this out," said Maureen, as she turned to the quilt. "This was hand-stitched."

"Hand-stitched? That's a good thing, right?"

"Not good, not bad, just a lot of work, something most people aren't willing to do nowadays. Leaves me in awe, it does. See how even and small the stitches are? That's the sign of a true craftsman, or, rather, craftswoman."

"That's sexist, Maureen. How can you be sure a man didn't make this?"

"I can't be. I'm just making an educated guess. Quilting wasn't traditionally man's work."

"I know guys who quilt," said Kate.

"The required sewing class in school doesn't count here."

"Maybe not, but even so . . . ."

"Just because something is acceptable now doesn't mean it was so in the past. When dealing with artifact identification, you have to start with what was historically typical. Of course, there are aberrations in history, people who didn't fit the mold for their gender or race or whatever, so a man could have made this quilt, but that's not likely. The most obvious scenario is that a woman did and she was probably a relative of the donor."

"How can you be sure?"

"The best way is to ask the donor," said Maureen. "Unfortunately, she slipped away before I could ask her anything specific about these things."

"Can't you call her?"

"That's my intention, once I get an inventory of the collection. I'll also ask who decorated the dress you like so much and, see these?" Maureen grabbed one of the receiving blankets and held it up for Kate to examine. "All the borders on these were done by hand, too. In this case, they were crocheted. Maybe our mysterious quilter was into other kinds of fiber arts and made these too."

"They're soft," said Kate. She ran her fingers over the flannel and pulled a corner to her cheek to rub it there. "Pee-yew!" She dropped the corner. "It smells like poop! Yuck! How can you stand it?"

"It's not so bad. We get musty, stinky stuff all the time. It doesn't usually smell like manure, though. These were stored in a barn. I'm going to take a bunch of it home to wash."

"I'm glad you get to do it, not me."

"Stick around here long enough, Kate, and you will get to do this stuff," said Maureen.

"No thanks. Got anything else in the box?"

"I don't think so, but let me check." Maureen glanced at the table the box had been on and started rifling through the clothes she had set there. "Wait a minute . . . where'd the booties go?"

"Booties?"

"Pink booties. They were right here." She lifted piles of clothing, trying to be ginger, though she was feeling frantic and wanted to fling them to the floor. "How could I have lost them? They were right here a minute ago."

"Take it easy, Maureen. They're here somewhere," said Kate. She set down her clipboard and started searching. "Maybe they're mixed into the clothes. If we take each piece and shake it out, one-by-one . . . then set them over here by the quilt, we'll find them."

"Good idea. Let's check under the quilt first." Maureen

picked it up and gently shook it. No booties. "As long as I'm
at it . . . grab me a clean garbage bag off the shelf behind my
desk, would you please, Kate?"

Kate did what was asked.

"I might as well get this out of the way," said Maureen,
as she folded the quilt and put it in the garbage bag for
future washing.

The women plucked through the clothing, intent on their
mission. Maureen shook the last pair of rubber pants in
frustration, their stiff crinkle giving no satisfaction. She was
almost in tears.

"Where could they be?" She rubbed her forehead hard
and squeezed her eyes shut. "They were right here . . . right
here. I can't believe I could be so dumb. I lost the booties."

Kate patted Maureen's back and said, "It's okay,
Maureen. They're just booties. They didn't up and walk
away."

Maureen laughed at Kate's inadvertent joke as two
small tears appeared at the corner of her eye. She swept
them away and said, "They very well could have . . . they're
booties."

Kate caught on. "Well, they're not gonna get far, 'cause
they're baby booties."

They shared a chuckle, which ended with a sigh from
Maureen. Kate half-sat on the edge of the now-empty table
while Maureen repacked the laundry bags.

"Why are you so broken up about them?" she asked.

"I'd rather not talk about it."

"Come on, Maureen. You practically go to pieces on me
and you're not going to dish? That is so not fair."

"It's not so much the booties as what they represent."

"You mean babies, don't you?"

"Yes, I mean babies," she said testily. Kate winced. "I'm
sorry, Kate. This is tough for me."

"How so?"

"I . . . well . . . I really want a baby."

"So have one. What's the big deal?"

"It's not that easy. I'm too old . . . ."

"Too old? You don't look that old to me. How old are you?"

"Forty-seven."

"Women can have babies in their forties, can't they?"

"Yes, but not me. I've already gone through menopause."

Kate considered this news for a moment and said, "You could pay a surrogate, or adopt."

"Is it just me, or are you high-schoolers getting smarter?"

"Hey, you've got options."

"And I've considered them, believe me. Problem is, I don't have a husband anymore."

"So?"

"I wouldn't feel right taking on a baby without a father around to help raise it."

"What century are you living in, Maureen? Look around you. Most of my friends are from broken homes, shuttling back-and-forth between Mom and Dad. I'm the weird one 'cause my folks are still together, but everyone else seems to be dealing with it. Besides, I bet you'd make a great mom."

"Thanks, Kate. That means a lot."

The clothes were repacked. Maureen turned to Kate, patted her on the head, and said, "Try to live without regret, dear. It's a heavy monkey to carry."

Kate picked at the cuff of her shorts, avoiding the gravity of the moment. "Yeah, yeah, *carpe diem* and all that. Dad's always saying stuff like that to me. Whatever." *Adults, why didn't they practice what they preached?* she thought.

"Now, what am I going to do about those booties?"

Kate bounced to her feet. "Why don't we ask Tatiana?"

"Tatiana?"

"I can't believe you haven't heard of Tatiana."

"Of course I've heard of Tatiana. You aren't buying that bunk about the museum being haunted by her, are you?"

"It's not bunk. Beverly feels her presence all the time. She's shown me pictures."

Here it comes, thought Maureen. Beverly was nice, but gullible. She reveled in sensational history – murders, robberies, kidnappings, ghost stories and natural disasters. As museum greeter, she felt it was her number one priority to inform visitors of The Great Ghost of Tatiana. She took a delicious morbid pride in relating how Tatiana, the former mistress of the mansion, had leapt to her death off the widow's walk. After the shudders and murmured exclamations subsided, Beverly would show visitors photos she'd captured of vapor wisps twirling above the front staircase, tell them of unexpected drafts of cold air, and explain how missing items magically appeared when Tatiana's spirit was invoked. As if wandering around the mansion's warren of rooms wasn't discombobulating enough, by the time Beverly was done with her tales, visitors would tiptoe around, glancing surreptitiously over their shoulders, and startle at the slightest floor squeak or movement caught out of the corner of an eye. Some loved the idea of a haunted house and would thunk around looking for Tatiana, practically ignoring the exhibits. Their exuberance was enough to convince a smart ghost to stay in hiding.

Maureen wasn't sure whether Tatiana's ghost drifted about the mansion – she remained noncommittal when pressed – but, ghost or no, she didn't appreciate Beverly's exploitation of the situation. It showed a flagrant disrespect for Tatiana and her husband, J. B. Watercott, who had willed the mansion to the City of Greenville some twenty-odd years back. Besides, there was more history in this town than the untimely death of Mrs. Tatiana Watercott.

"Don't look at me like that, Maureen," said Kate.

"Like what?"

"Like I'm a crazy, stupid teenager. Besides, how is asking Tatiana any different than Mom running around the house praying to St. Anthony to find her lost keys?"

"You've got a point there. At least with Tatiana we won't have to put an ad in the paper for prayers answered."

"Okay, here goes." Kate stood erect, held her arms out

to her sides with palms up, lifted her face to the ceiling, and closed her eyes. "Oh, Great Tatiana! With profound earnestness, we entreat you to find the pair of pink baby booties that Maureen lost. We will be forever grateful for your assistance – won't we, Maureen?" Maureen nodded, trying to remain serious as Kate finished with a sound "amen" and a few "ohms."

A shadow flicked across Kate's tennis shoe. "Holy crap! What was that?"

"Not Tatiana, if that's what you're thinking," replied Maureen. "We've got a mouse. Have you checked the traps?"

"Where'd he go?" Kate moved in the direction of the collections shelves and hunkered low to spot the rodent.

"The important question is where'd he come from? We have to be sure there aren't more." Maureen headed for the most likely suspect, the empty box. There'd been enough mouse dirt inside for a colony. She tried not to dwell on the fact that the mouse had probably been in the box while she'd been fishing around in it. She grabbed a corner of the box and slowly pulled it out from under the table.

"Well, lookee here!" she said.

"What?"

"The booties, they're on the floor. I must've shoved them off the table while I was working on the clothes."

"High-five, Maureen! Tatiana came through. Do you believe in her now?"

"The evidence is still too circumstantial for me."

"Come on. You promised you'd be forever grateful."

"I'm grateful, alright, but maybe I owe it to the mouse."

"Suit yourself. I'm not taking any chances." Kate assumed her previous ritualistic stance and said, "I thank you, Great Tatiana, for helping find the baby booties. If you want to take out your wrath on anyone, just make sure it's Maureen and not me. Amen."

"Kate! How could you? Setting me up for a curse."

"Hey, you're the unbeliever. It shouldn't be a problem

for you."

"Isn't it about time you finish checking the temp and humidity?" Maureen handed Kate her clipboard. "Now, skedaddle. And, if you see Norman, send him up to deal with the mouse."

"Got it," said Kate, as she made note of the figures she had come for. Then, she disappeared down the staircase.

Maureen zipped the booties into a plastic baggie, thereby making them harder to lose, and put the baggie with the rest of the clothing. She sat at her desk wondering how to finish up the day. It was too late to start anything big.

Her mind drifted to her reaction concerning the booties. As curator, she often found herself getting attached to particular artifacts. She and her colleagues in the museum field worked hard to pack and organize objects, handling them with mindfulness, learning their histories, and sensing the auras of their past owners. The maternal instinct was natural and fierce among curators. Given this, misplacing artifacts was worrisome, but with the thousands of items entrusted to her care, it was also inevitable. Normally, she could take the temporary loss of an object in stride, but she'd been downright panicked over the booties. Damn that Alex, anyway.

Mister Devil May Care and Curly Hair had been her husband once upon a regrettable time. She never understood what he found appealing in her. His fine features didn't match her stocky ones. He was lush, with lines of an Adonis. She, with her granite chin, thin hair, and stout birthing hips, was stupidly flattered.

She never got to test her hips. Alex kept putting her off, even though she'd been clear that she wanted children. "Now's not the time, dear. Now's not the time." It became time after he'd left her for some hotty-totty slip of a girl with no boobs, no butt, and no hips. Nice hair, though, and gorgeous topaz eyes. Maureen couldn't work up the typical shunned wife's hate for Alex's new wife, even though she got the two children Maureen wanted. Alex was a different story. She reserved her disdain for this man who wouldn't shit or get off the pot and had consequently dashed her big dream to the ground in much the same way that Tatiana had met her end.

The suicide door came slowly into focus. Maureen's chair had swiveled 'round to face the door, which was behind her desk. It was nailed shut with two-by-four cross beams and led to a now non-existent widow's walk. According to the Greenville rumor circuit, Mr. Watercott had tended to this task himself, not leaving it to some hired hand. The two-by-fours were meticulously affixed with more large carpenter's nails than were necessary. As upset as he had reportedly been when he had discovered his wife's body, he was not a hasty man and this was not a hasty job. Maureen wondered what had been going through his mind as he measured the boards, sawed them to length, and hammered them into place.

Maureen had never been able to definitively prove the reason for Tatiana's escape, but she had her theories. By reading between the lines of the historic record, she'd been able to pick up the hidden insinuations of the Watercotts' lives. J. B., also known as "Buster," was Joseph Bennington Watercott. Maureen didn't understand the Victorian convention wherein men went by their initials. It sounded so yacht club. Greenville could hardly be considered yacht club territory, what with the shallow, often lethargic Mud River. "Buster" didn't fit, either. It was too frat house or young boy to be appropriate. J. B. must have realized this because he only allowed his closest business associates to use the nickname with him.

J. B. came to Greenville in 1914 to open a bank. He was a ripe twenty-five and already owned several banks in nearby villages. He had a business partner, a man whose name Maureen couldn't recall. She did remember the partner being a shady character with whom J. B. eventually parted ways.

Greenville had been an industrious town in the early

1900s and J. B. made a healthy fortune from the bank and his real estate deals. Maureen had followed the hot pursuit of J. B. by various young ladies in the local columns of the newspaper. Of course, the columns weren't blatant about these tender affections, but the swirl of parties and outings of the town's most eligible bachelor made for good copy and Maureen had been studying history long enough to know that some things don't change. The museum's collections included a handful of cabinet photos of J. B. from this time period. He was dreamy with his hooded eyes and dark handlebar moustache.

While he didn't lack for potential wives, J. B. remained unmarried into his early thirties. It was about this time that he took a business trip to Europe. When he returned to Greenville, Tatiana was on his arm, a Russian beauty who could barely spit out a word of English. How Tatiana and J. B. communicated was beyond Maureen, but J. B. doted on his wife. He built her this house, adding the widow's walk to her specifications so that she could look out over the river.

Because of the language barrier and her ethnicity, which was too exotic by Greenville's standards, Tatiana had difficulty mixing with the other high society ladies in town. Parties were held in the house, plenty of them early on, but they only served to breed jealousy among the less fortunate of the upper class. Tatiana's naturally quiet demeanor did nothing to ease the ruffling of these gossipy fancy chickens, who picked at her and called her the Siberian Queen. The local papers didn't print any of this. They were sensitive to a lady's virtues, especially when the lady was the wife of J.B. Watercott. Maureen gathered these tidbits from a woman who was the daughter of one of the Watercotts' housekeepers and had lived in the house as a child.

After a while, the house parties stopped and Maureen lost the public thread of the Watercotts' private lives. It picked up again when she found an article about the birth of the Watercotts' first child, a seemingly healthy baby boy. Two months later, the boy died of unknown causes.

From the description in the paper, Maureen figured it had been a SIDS death. The baby was buried on the Watercott estate and lay under a stone with both Russian and English epitaphs.

There were other stones grouped with the baby's, among them Tatiana's and J. B.'s, as well as a couple of small, flat markers with a single date on each, and another larger stone inscribed to an infant. Maureen searched the newspapers around the dates given on the flat markers and found one small clue. About a week after one of the dates, it was reported that Tatiana had taken to her bed. Strange how this was considered appropriate fodder for the local columns, a single cryptic sentence on a health issue with no wider explanation. Maureen wondered if Tatiana had twice miscarried, enduring the tragedies as best she could and managing, for the most part, to keep them out of the public eye.

The other infant stone was for Baby Evva, who had died at seven months of diphtheria. Within the year, her mother leapt to her death. It wasn't difficult to see why, but Maureen had also run across a copy of a probate record showing that Tatiana had been committed to an insane asylum within a month of Evva's birth. The record described symptoms that matched those of postpartum depression, but was not recognized as such at the time.

Given the circumstances, Maureen would've jumped, too. She'd been tempted after Alex had left and then again when menopause became a certainty. During her unsettled moments, the door hulked over her, ready to suck her through and hawk her out on the other side. She'd spent many nauseous months learning to desensitize herself to its horrifying power. To cope, she thanked J. B. profusely for blockading the door. Time, the prayers to J. B., and an appreciation of her fertile imagination got her through and dismantled her fear. The door was just a door – a door whose history could now be considered with little emotion.

Maureen pulled her eyes away from it and searched out

her clock radio. It was after five – past closing. Norman
would be waiting to lock up. She grabbed her things and
bustled down the stairs to find Norman holding the back
door for her.

"Got some things to wash up, Ms. Lestico?" he said as
she went through.

"Yes, Norman. We'll see you Tuesday. Oh, and see if
you can find that mouse."

"Good enough, Ms. Lestico."

Maureen shifted the bags in her hands to a comfortable position for walking and headed toward the river. She
paused near the water and surveyed the opposite shore.
The sun over her shoulder winked in the siding of the Tin
Man's house, turning the crushed pop cans into hundreds
of crinkly, star-bright eyes. It was a real work of art, but few
shared her opinion. Most Greenville residents couldn't wait
to have it torn down. The kindest among them called it a
shack. The rest called it a dump, or worse. She knew the
prissy, tidy ones would win and one day soon, the house
would be unceremoniously demolished. Leroy Jarbeau was
a walking artifact, descended as he was from one of the earli-
est Greenville settlers, a fur trader named François Jarbeau.
Leroy's house, which had no electricity or indoor plumbing,
was the last of a vanishing way of life in Greenville, yet, because Leroy was poor, his home was destined for a landfill.

Maureen looked back at the Watercott mansion. The
façade, three solid stories of red brick set in Flemish bond
courses, proclaimed its place on the perimeter of the old
industrial district. The perfection of this side of the house
was marred only by the slight interruption of the newer
brickwork used to patch the place where the widow's walk
had once hung. The door to nowhere floated in unanchored
misery above.

Inside, the mansion was outfitted with the finest
amenities – mahogany paneling, darkly stained rock maple
floors, ornate crown moldings and trim, picture rails, Middle
Eastern rugs, a music room with stained glass windows,

hand carved banisters, and velvety floral wall papers. No
detail was overlooked in its design, right down to the key-
hole plates stamped with the Watercott symbol, a standing
bear catching water drops in an outstretched paw. Of course
there was plumbing and electricity, along with steam heat.
The servants' quarters were palaces in comparison to the Tin
Man's house, but that did not diminish The Tin Man's accomplishment. He had built his home himself, bartering and
scrounging for building materials with no cadre of profes-
sionals to do his bidding.

Maureen glanced once more at the suicide door, and
then again at the Tin Man's house, and set off through the
former industrial district on the west bank of the Mud River.
The old mills and other structures were gone for the most
part. Trees and sharp, thigh-high grasses had reclaimed the
riverside. Maureen was aware of the remnants of some hidden foundations mixed among the thick underbrush. The
odd red brick turned up now and again along the single-
file dirt trail that had been worn through the area. The city
didn't care to expend the effort to keep the industrial district
mowed because it wanted to discourage people from using
it. These efforts were for naught and actually made the district more inviting, especially to partying young people.

Maureen "tsk, tsked" at the crumpled chip wrappers,
crushed pop bottles, and rancid beer cans she encountered
as she made her way home along the path. It wasn't that
she minded the idea of people having a little fun. She just
wished they'd take their junk with them when they were
done. The easier and cleaner route would've been the sidewalk, but Maureen liked how the view of the river and hint
of wilderness in the city cleared her mind of the day's work.
Litter notwithstanding, of course.

The half-way point between the museum and home was
marked with a giant storm water runoff drain set back from
the river's edge. Fully grown men, stooping just a bit, could
stand inside the cement conduit. In wet years, the drain was
a small waterfall, situated as it was about ten feet above the

shoreline. In flood years, the pipe and river convened in a romantic tryst and exchanged fluids. This was a dry year, however, and Maureen would be able to walk underneath the drain, rather than climb up and over.

As she neared the drain, her ears pricked to an odd, yet familiar noise. She halted, silencing the rustle of the laundry bags. She cocked her head and listened closely. Nothing. No sooner did she move, the noise resumed. It was coming from the river. Maureen scanned the water while trying to place the sound.

It was George, or rather, the horrendous yowl he had made when Maureen had accidentally slammed his tail in the screen door the previous spring. Hearing the same piteous sound now, her heart twisted beneath her breast. She had to make it stop.

There. Right there. In the river, not more than a few feet off shore, was a black trash bag hung up on a piece of driftwood.

"Kittens! Goddamnit! What is wrong with people?"

Maureen dropped everything and shot down the bank and into the water.

She untangled the bag from the driftwood and dragged it to shore. She tore it open and immediately stopped thinking.

She wasn't sure how she had managed to get the baby home, much less change it out of its wet clothes and into those she had been carrying. The clothes, girl clothes, weren't really appropriate for the river baby, who was a boy. A baby boy. He was sleeping in her arms, stunned and exhausted from his ordeal.

Maureen felt biblical as she rocked the baby in her cushy, slate blue recliner. God had answered her prayers, sending her a baby via the Mud River, her very own Moses. Although a reed basket was a kinder way to travel than a trash bag. She'd have to reassess her indifference toward God, who'd certainly never been one to respond to her prayers, not until this particular moment, anyway.

George didn't care for the baby. He'd sniffed the child's pulsating soft spot and hidden away in a huff in the laundry room. She'd have to kiss up to him for a long time after this situation resolved itself. George was good at holding grudges.

Maureen knew she couldn't keep the baby. Her rational brain was telling her to call the police and report the incident. Her toddler brain was whining, "It's my baby and you can't have him! Finders keepers, losers weepers."

Who would throw away a perfectly good baby? This one looked to be a few months old. He'd been carefully dressed in a powder blue pantsuit and white vest, suitable enough for a baptismal ceremony. Why go to all the trouble to dress a throwaway baby in such a fine outfit?

She watched the hollows form and disappear under his round cheeks as he sucked his tongue, softly smacking it against his palate. He looked like he was eating, which reminded Maureen that he was going to wake up hungry. She had to figure out how to feed him without letting anyone know she had him. She couldn't just stroll into the local Wal-Mart with an infant and purchase a carton of formula, let alone diapers or clothing. The superstore was the Grand Central of social relationships and someone was sure to recognize her. Even if she could find a store where she was anonymous, how would she get the baby there without a car seat? The questions about her predicament kept coming, not allowing her to rest and enjoy the baby's peace. How was she going to explain this to her co-workers, her neighbors, her friends? What was she going to do about work? What about the mother of this child? What if she wanted him back? Was taking the baby illegal?

The baby wriggled in his sleep. He was a sweet one, this baby boy. Sweet and warm and . . . wet? Jesus. He'd peed on her. Maureen wriggled, too, and woke the baby, who started crying. She shushed him, lifting herself and the baby out of the recliner. The front of her shirt and pants were soaked, while the baby continued to gush. From the volume of liquid issuing forth, it appeared as though he had absorbed several gallons of river water.

"Diaper change, darling," said Maureen. She swung him through the air at arm's length, letting his wetness drip on the floor instead of on her. Through the kitchen and into the laundry room, the baby continued his squall as she went for a towel in the linen closet. She rested the baby on her hip as she retrieved the towel and a washcloth. Automatically, she adopted a mommy rock and sway, a habit she'd picked up during her two years spent as an *au pair* after college. Her hips were good for something after all, maybe not birthing, but this would do.

She ran the washcloth under hot water from the laundry room sink. George eyed her with evil slits and hissed as she placed first the towel and then the baby on the clothes folding counter. "Stop being such a fussbudget, George," she said.

"It's okay, honey. You're okay," she cooed at the baby, who had balled up his fists and pulled in his legs. He was crying with such exertion that he could barely make a sound. His face was pinched and fuchsia.

Maureen pulled off his wet pants and laughed. She'd forgotten to put a diaper on after rescuing him. Damned stupid for a former nanny. She was reduced to a movie cliché – an inept bachelor forced to take care of an infant, unable to do even the simplest things, like put on a disposable diaper. Only she didn't have disposable diapers. She had Nancy Pettey's cloth diapers. Diapers that rightfully belonged to the Watercott Museum. She tasted sour guilt, but chose to ignore it. Given the circumstances, it was more important to worry about the baby than the museum. She was sure Nancy would understand. She picked up the baby and jiggled him while sifting through the mound of clothing on top of the dryer. She didn't remember having emptied the bags.

The baby hiccupped and sniffled in between screechy outbursts. She couldn't blame him, suffering as he was from the indignity of a bare butt hanging out in the breeze. She plucked a diaper, rubber pants and a pair of khaki twill pants from the heap, getting a whiff of barn and mold in the process. She wished she could wash everything before putting it on the baby.

Maureen wrapped the boy in a towel and cradled him in her arms. "Let's go sightseeing," she said with a lilt, "We need safety pins." The baby calmed to listen.

"This is the laundry room, of course. Here's the dryer and the washing machine, and under the laundry tub, see?" Maureen bent over to give the baby a better view. "There's my kitty again. Say hi to George." She assisted the baby by waving his fist at the cat.

A mouthless growl reverberated from the back of George's throat and the svelte marmalade turned to face the wall.

"He's just a baby, George. He won't hurt you."

George repeated the growl.

"Fine. Have it your way," said Maureen. She turned back to the baby and walked out of the laundry room.

"This is the hallway, and behind that door is my office. You can peek inside, but I really shouldn't let you because it's a terrible mess. Do you think there are any safety pins in here?"

The baby blew bubbles in response.

"That's what I thought. Too much work to find them. There might be some in my bedroom. Shall we go look?"

She set the baby on the bed, keeping a hand on him while she searched her bed stand drawer, eventually finding a few stray safety pins mixed with her scrappy reading notes, ball-point pens, paper clips, bobby pins, a tube of floral-scented hand cream, fruity lip balm, and a deck of tarot cards from her friend Araminta.

"Okay, baby, time to get dressed. Maureen changed

the baby while he copied the expressions on her face –
furrowing a brow here, rounding his mouth there, looking
away briefly when the interaction got too intense.

"I suppose, sweet cheeks, we should come up with a
name for you. I can't call you 'baby' forever. What do you
think of that?" She gave him a smile and he reciprocated.

"I'll take that for agreement," she said as she skooched
on the rubber pants. "A name . . . a name . . . a name for the
baby," she sang. "How about Moses?"

The baby's lip quavered.

"Don't cry, honey. We can pick something else. Hmmm
. . . Steve? Patrick? Quincy? . . . Quincy? Where'd I get
that? Yuck. . . . I want a name that means something. I
found you in the river . . . . Bob. No, not Bob. That'd be
cruel. I could call you River, but that's too hippy dippy."

The baby was losing interest, so Maureen repeated
"hippy dippy" in a silly voice and gave him tummy
raspberries while she thought.

"I've got it . . . how about Reed? You may not have come
to me in a reed basket, but we can pretend you did."

The baby gave her a lop-sided spitty smile.

"Reed it is." Maureen picked him up and kissed his
velvety cheek. She placed him in the center of the bed, so he
wouldn't roll off, and changed out of her pee-soaked clothes,
the very ones she had been wearing when she'd gone into
the river. Why she had not thought to remove them, especially the muddy damp pants, was beyond her. What else
had she missed in those brief moments following the baby's
rescue?

"I don't have time for this," she said to herself. To Reed,
she said, "Let's figure out what to feed you. Dr. Spock might
have some ideas."

Maureen took Reed into her office, where she was
storing boxes of old books. She had gotten a copy of Dr.
Benjamin Spock's *Baby and Child Care* from her mother when
she was hired as an *au pair*. She was hoping she still had it.

The boxes were on a high shelf in the closet. She

couldn't hold the baby while retrieving the boxes, but she wasn't keen on laying him directly on the floor, either.

"I'd give anything for a car seat, Reed. What are we going to do with you? .... Let's see. .... This isn't insurmountable. We just have to use our imagination."

Sailing between rooms with Reed in the crook of her arm, Maureen assembled an ad hoc seat for the baby using a laundry basket and folded comforter. Once he was safely deposited, she sorted through the boxes, chattering to Reed as she did so. He was better company than George, and soon she found the book she sought.

"Just as I suspected. There's a formula recipe here that'll do the trick. Evaporated milk, water and corn syrup. Simple enough. Let me mark this . . . page 143 . . . and we'll see if we've got what we need."

A brief stop in the laundry room to throw in a load of baby clothes, and back to the kitchen she went, with Reed riding in his basket. It occurred to Maureen that she hadn't gotten this much mileage out of her house in a long time.

She found five cans of evaporated milk and a half a bottle of corn syrup in a kitchen cupboard. "This should get us by for a little while, huh, Reed?"

She opened a can of milk and poured it into a pot on the stove. She added the water and corn syrup and turned on the heat, stirring periodically until the mixture came to a boil. George made an appearance, squinting. His nose wriggled in the air, catching the scent of the milk.

"That's all it took? A little milk?"

"Marawr," replied George.

"This is for the baby, but we can spare you some. Can't we, Reed?"

George ignored the baby, who was becoming restive and whiny in his basket. Instead, the cat rubbed up against Maureen's legs, twining through them.

"Not now, George. The baby's hungry and I have to cool this fast." She nudged the cat away with her foot and put the pan on a potholder in the fridge.

"Shit!"

Reed startled with the expletive, his whine switching to a full-fledged wail. George skittered back to the laundry room.

"No bottles. There are no baby bottles. How am I supposed to feed you?" Maureen looked at the baby, suddenly afraid to pick him up. "This was too easy. I should've known God would screw this up for me. What am I going to do?" Maureen felt her own wail welling up.

Reed reached desperation pitch before she did. She coughed, temporarily expelling her fear of failing him, fetched him from the basket, and rocked him for all she was worth.

She would have to call someone. Blow her secret. How dare God do this to her? Send her a baby; make sure she had almost everything she needed, but not the damn baby bottles? She careened about the kitchen, Reed bawling and perched on a hip while she opened cupboards and drawers looking for a possible solution. She found George's old medicine syringe, but dismissed it as a last ditch potentiality. It was too small and there might be residue that would harm the baby. She considered a cup, but the baby was too young to have much control with it. She saw a stray rubber glove in a drawer and mulled its possibilities. If she poked a needle hole into a finger, she might be able to feed Reed like a calf. It was silly, she knew, but she was running out of options. She was tempted to try a prayer to the Great Tatiana.

"Darn it, Reed! Stop crying! I'm doing the best I can."

Reed did not stop, but registered her agitation by turning up the volume.

"I'm sorry, Reed. That wasn't fair." Maureen brought his face to hers and kissed his forehead. "We're in this together, baby, and my flipping out isn't helping, is it? Let's try to calm down and see if something comes to us. . . . . Oh! Look! A birdie out the window."

The change in Maureen's tone and the distraction brought Reed's storm down to a gentle pitter. As they watched the birds flitter around the feeder out the kitchen window, something blue on the counter by the sink caught Maureen's attention. It was the pop-up cover of a water bottle. Normally, she discarded these when she readied the bottles for recycling, but this one hadn't made it to the garbage can.

Maureen's brain clicked. It might work. She could regulate the flow by keeping the pop top slightly closed. All she needed was the empty bottle. She took Reed outside to the recycling bin sitting against the house by the backdoor and fished around the plastics with one arm until she found the bottle. She grabbed another just in case and brought Reed back inside to wash them.

The baby was starting to fuss again. Maureen put him back in the basket, the last place he wanted to be at that particular moment.

"I'll be right with you, darling. You poor thing. I'm so cruel to put you in that little basket while you're starving to death." Maureen poured the homemade formula into a bottle and capped it. "Okay, sweetie, time to eat."

She swept the baby, basket and all, into the living room, scooped the baby into her arms and plopped into the recliner to feed him. After a bit of adjustment with the pop top and no small amount of dribbling, Maureen and Reed found a rhythm that worked sufficiently well to transfer milk from bottle to stomach and the baby fed until he fell asleep.

Maureen and Reed spent the night in the chair, Maureen's night being the more restless of the two. She'd doze, then wake with a start, thinking the baby had slipped from her arms or had suffocated at her bosom. She wondered at her good fortune and her ability to become hopelessly attached to someone she had known for less than a day. She'd die for Reed without hesitation. Sleeplessness wasn't an issue.

Sunday came. Maureen threw herself happily into the endless tasks associated with baby care. Feeding, changing, making formula, shooing jealous George away, washing laundry with no thought to separating the loads as she should have, singing and jabbering to Reed and enjoying his pliable facial expressions and uncoordinated hand movements. The day was interrupted by a call from Araminta, who wanted to get together for tea and a chat, but Maureen begged off with the excuse that she was coming down with something. Sunday went.

Monday was more of the same. Maureen took Reed into the backyard for a fresh air foray, but only because the backyard was relatively secluded by a fence and high hedges. She realized that she was avoiding television and radio and hadn't even read the daily paper for fear that the authorities would be looking for the baby. Araminta called again to inquire as to her health and to offer care and comfort. Maureen said in her best stuffy-nosed accent, "Danks, but dat won'd be necessary. I jes need some resd."

Tuesday was a work day. Maureen called in sick, making Beverly's day by adding grist to her gossip mill. She hadn't missed work in years for an illness and had amassed the maximum number of sick days. These, along with some unused vacation days, would buy her a month-and-a-half with Reed. Time off was easy to calculate. It was keeping up the premise of an illness for that amount of time that scared Maureen. Eventually people were bound to become suspicious and drop by in order to assure themselves that she wasn't suffering from cancer or some other life threatening ailment. Besides, her coworkers would soon miss her for a more practical reason. They would quickly be inundated with new donations to the collections. Without Maureen, the artifacts would pile up in unaccessioned heaps until they were unmanageable.

George began warming up to Reed on Tuesday, if only because he knew that whenever the baby ate, he was treated to a small dish of formula. Maureen noted that she was running low on evaporated milk, having maybe one day's supply left. She'd deal with that when the time came.

Wednesday brought another call to work and another lie

about her condition. Reed squawked during her conversation with Beverly. Maureen had to lie about that, too, using George as her patsy. Maureen had never been a good liar, especially in person. Her body language gave her away. At least with the telephone and Beverly's credulity, she had a shot at being believed, but the dishonesty led to paranoia.

She spent the day with the front drapes closed, which compounded the feeling that soon her secret would be blown. She moved slowly and quietly around the house with Reed, willing the universe to pay her and her baby no heed.

In the afternoon, they sat in the recliner looking through a visual dictionary. Maureen whispered what she knew about bowler hats and spats and starched collars to Reed, who took everything quite seriously. By late afternoon, he was napping. Maureen moved him to her bed and lay down next to him.

She was three winks from sleep when the doorbell rang. Maureen felt like a jackrabbit trapped by wolves, a sensation exacerbated by the sudden waking. Her heart rattled in her rib cage and blood throbbed in her ears. She gathered what senses she could and inched herself off the bed, so as not to disturb Reed.

The bedroom window looked out upon the front door. Maureen peeped through a gap between the drapes. She saw Kate standing on her stoop, ready to hit the bell again. Donning a robe and slippers, she made sure Reed was still sleeping. She headed to the bathroom, where she mussed her hair, shoved a handful of tissues into her robe pocket and took a quick sniff of mentholated cold rub, enough to make her eyes water. Kate rang again. Maureen shut the bedroom door on her way to answering the front door.

She cracked it open. "Hi, Kate."

"You look terrible," Kate said.

"I feel terrible. Don't be offended if I don't ask you in. I don't want you catching what I've got."

"What is it, the flu, or something?"

"I think so," said Maureen. She wiped her nose for effect.

"We really miss you at work."

"Already? I haven't been gone that long."

"No, but some guy brought in a box of photos. They're pretty cool. And a lady donated an old head scarf her great-great grandmother wore when she immigrated, plus a bunch of books."

"It never ends, does it?" said Maureen. George came up behind her and mewed. Thinking it was the baby, Maureen jumped. Her hand shook as she tried to cover her surprise with another nose wipe.

"Are you gonna be okay?" said Kate.

"I'll be fine," said Maureen. "A few more days of rest ought to cure me."

"I better get going, then," said Kate. "Is there anything I can get you?"

Here it was, the answer to Maureen's next dilemma presenting itself to her. "If you wouldn't mind," she said, "George could use more evaporated milk. I'm not going to be able to get to the store for a few days . . . ." This was an easy lie.

"Sure, no problem. How many cans d'ya need?"

"Five . . . no, make it ten."

"Ten cans?" Kate bent to scratch George's head. "You're going to be one fat kitty."

The cat sat compliantly at Maureen's feet. He was all for the promise of evaporated milk formula.

"Wait here while I get some money." Maureen dashed into the bedroom while Kate was busy with George. Reed slept on. She rummaged through her purse for some bills and presented them to Kate at the door.

"Do you have time to get it and bring it back this evening?" she asked Kate. "I'm almost out."

"Can it be after supper?"

"That'll be fine. Thanks for stopping by. I'm going to nap for a while."

"See you later," said Kate, and mercifully, she was gone.

Maureen went back to the bedroom and lay with Reed until he woke. Napping was out of the question. She had to figure out the logistics of Kate's return.

Supper came and went. Around eight, Kate arrived. Reed was not sleeping this time, so Maureen put him in his basket in her bedroom before answering the door.

"Here you go. Ten cans of evaporated milk and change."

"That's great. Thanks, Kate."

"Did you hear?"

"What?"

"There's a baby missing," said Kate.

Maureen's stomach dropped. "Really?" she said. Suddenly, she felt truly sick.

"A girl who used to go to my school – she'd be a sophomore this year if she was still coming – she had the baby a few months ago. She didn't want to take care of it anymore and threw it in the river."

"Oh, my." Maureen didn't know what else to say.

"They're dredging the river," Kate continued.

"I think you need to leave, Kate."

"Are you gonna throw up? You're looking a little green."

"Yes, that's it. Go on. I'll see you soon," said Maureen. She practically shut the door in Kate's face, dropped the milk and change in the entry and ran to the bedroom, where she held Reed as tightly as she could.

The light of Thursday morning eased the sharp fear of the previous evening. Maureen made another batch of formula for Reed, as she had the past several mornings, and talked herself into carrying on as though none of it had happened.

She washed the baby clothes that had been Nancy's, but were now Reed's. Her favorite outfit for Reed was the pair of strawberry pants with a red t-shirt. They played with George and watched birds at the feeder. She considered taking Reed to the backyard, but decided against the idea.

Feeding, napping, changing, a blessedly normal day.

Maureen and Reed had settled into the recliner for another session with the visual dictionary when the doorbell rang. Into the basket and back to the bedroom went Reed. Maureen was already schlumping around in her robe, knowing that another visit from museum staff was inevitable. She'd lie her way through this, too.

When she answered the door, there stood Araminta, who said simply, "You have to give him back, Maureen."

d

Story 6

Spotless

This was to be no pleasure cruise through Wal-Mart. Nancy had a full day's work ahead of her. She disentangled one gray cart from another in the cart stall and moved it out of the stream of Saturday morning shoppers so that she could peruse her list. Danny had warned her that she would need something stronger than the baking soda and vinegar she liked to use. She was tentatively taking his word that the products he suggested wouldn't be overkill.

Murphy's Oil Soap . . . pine cleaner . . . dish soap . . . Comet . . . glass cleaner with ammonia . . . Drāno or Liquid Plumber. (He'd been clear that the tub and sink were impossibly clogged, but thought these were worth a try before hiring a plumber to come with a snake.) The list continued . . . bleach ("But don't use it with ammonia, or you'll die.") . . . sponges . . . heavy-duty terrycloth rags ("If you can't find them in cleaning supplies, check automotive.") . . . a mop with a couple of extra heads . . . a scrub brush or two . . . a plunger ("I broke Mom's. Did I forget to mention that the toilet's plugged, too?") . . . paper towels . . . a toilet brush ("Really, Nancy, you are not going to want to reach into it.") . . . trash bags . . . toothbrushes with stiff bristles . . . a bucket ("No, get two, in fact, double everything on the list – you won't regret it.") . . . and Greased Lightning.

Greased Lightning? This was going too far. They were cleaning Mom's house, not an industrial kitchen slimed over with bacon fat encapsulating twenty years of particulate matter. Greased Lightning stunk to high heaven, the smell strong enough to strip an esophagus. A couple of sprays and any filth, no matter how baked on or imbedded, would run screaming from the chemical. Nancy had argued with Danny over this one. Wouldn't some bathroom wipes do the job? Besides, the chemical soup from all this stuff was sure to grow an instantaneous tumor, or, at the very least, an eleventh toe. Danny was insistent. He had said, "Mom's house is not like you remember it." After losing the argument, Nancy added rubber gloves and a face mask to her list. She hoped she wouldn't need a ventilator.

Nancy mentally mapped her route through the store and took off down a main aisle, which was blocked by racks of clearance items.

How typical, she thought - *busiest shopping day of the week, and store management makes it even more difficult to get around.* A three-dollar sweater in a fuzzy periwinkle cable-knit beckoned her. She ignored it, tooling through the clothing and rounding the corner near the shoes. As she made a left, she looked right and spotted one of her kindergartners in the shoe department, racks towering above him.

He saw her, too. "Hi, Mrs. Pettey! How do you like my shoes?" He had on a pair of sparkling pink mules and lifted a heel demurely so she could get a look at the top.

"They're lovely, Leroy, especially with the athletic socks."

"You're such a kidder, Mrs. Pettey. I would never wear these with socks."

"Of course not. You're much too fashionable for that."

He beamed a halogen smile.

"See you later, Leroy."

"Bye, Mrs. Pettey." He went back to his shoes while Nancy buzzed over to cleaning supplies.

She jockeyed for a place among several zombie shoppers, who were oblivious to her attempts to grab what she needed. Why couldn't people pay attention to what was going on around them?

Despite battling with the hordes, Nancy completed her hunter-gatherer session in record time, arriving at the checkout in forty-five minutes. She had been lucky. Normally, a trip to Wal-Mart was an exercise in social networking in which she couldn't escape seeing a half-dozen people she knew who wanted to stop and chat.

In her rush to the parking lot, Nancy almost ran over an old man with her cart. He was carrying a violin case and wearing a long overcoat, even though the day was a comfortable 70 degrees Fahrenheit. He tipped his hat to her and said, "Pardon me, ma'am," as if their near collision had been his fault.

"Oh, no, no, pardon me," she said. "I wasn't paying attention."

"You're forgiven," he said, "Although, you wouldn't have to apologize if I hadn't been right where you wanted to be." He shifted his weight from one foot to the other.

Odd, Nancy thought. His shoes don't match. Leroy would have something to say about that.

"Say what," the man continued, "Seeing as how you've apologized for your part, I'm sorry for my part."

He stuck out a hand and Nancy shook it, saying, "That's okay." His hand lingered an ounce longer than propriety dictated. Nancy felt a desperation for human connection in the grasp and quickly shook free, saying, "I have to get going. Have a good day."

"Good day to you, ma'am."

As she loaded her purchases into the minivan, she furtively looked back toward the store and saw that the old man had taken a seat on an outdoor bench, his violin resting beside him. He looked familiar now that she saw him from this distance, but she couldn't place him. He waved and greeted people as they entered and exited the store. He seemed to know a lot of people, many of whom appeared to know him right back. Maybe she'd just imagined his loneliness. She'd have to ask Danny who he was.

She drove her way through the madhouse that was the Lime Street shopping district, maneuvering around tentative drivers and deftly dodging a white Cadillac that threatened to T-bone her.

When the Lime Street Bridge, "The Limey," as it was known to locals, had been built some ten to fifteen years prior, the City Council, at the insistence of the county highway engineer, voted on a plan to widen all of Lime Street and make it a major thoroughfare. The four-laner soon attracted new business development, which resulted in heavy traffic in what used to be the outskirts of town. Greenville's downtown business owners weren't pleased. Nancy couldn't understand why. Wasn't economic expansion a good thing? Danny kept her up-to-date on the latest gripes from town. He heard it all at the butcher shop, even though he was in the pro-development camp. Nancy could picture him calmly carving a quarter of beef while some testy shrew unloaded on him, hoping to change his mind. When the complainer finished, Danny would say, "There's no sense competing with them directly. You've gotta offer something they can't give," and he'd drop his cleaver through a bony part of the meat, allowing it to thump the counter as punctuation. He was unflappable, a good trait for a guy swinging sharp objects, a trait that Nancy was depending on to get her through cleaning her mother's house.

The Spolvero farm was about seven miles east of Greenville on County Road 29. It had seemed farther out when Nancy was a kid. Because she had lived on a farm, she rarely got to have friends over, while all the townie kids were forever getting together for makeup and hair parties, or games of Red Rover and Kick the Can.

As she approached the farm, she saw the row of pines that her father had planted as a barrier between the yard and the highway. When she got closer, she could make out three sandy pink boulders that marked the front corner of the property. She and her siblings had spent many an afternoon playing lookout atop the rocks, diving down behind them as vehicles approached. One time, Dad caught them throwing gravel into the road from this corner, or, rather, he caught Mike, who happened to be in mid-pitch. A spanking behind the house followed. Knowing the probable guilt of the others, Dad made the rest of them watch as he slid the belt out of his belt loops, doubled it over, leather on leather, and snapped it. Three times he laid it across Mike's backside. Three times Nancy flinched as Mike flinched, feeling worse for having to witness the punishment than Mike did for having to take it.

Thankfully, spankings with the belt were infrequent. Nancy could think of only a few other times besides the gravel incident, and she had never been at the receiving end. Dad was normally a pushover, at least with her, and didn't get after the kids much. It was Mom you had to watch out for.

Nancy turned off the highway and onto the dirt road that led to the farm's ringed driveway. She pulled in, parking close to the house. Danny hadn't arrived, yet. He had the key. Even if she'd been in possession of one, she wasn't about to go in without her brother. Not with years of avoidance on her side.

She got out of the minivan and walked along the driveway, noting changes since her last visit. There was a white silage tube next to the first barn. Nancy preferred old-fashioned silos to these giant, bloated gut-spilling grub worms. That's what they reminded her of, anyway. Leave it to Danny to get one. He liked to taunt the girls with grubs when he was little, once putting one down the back of Nancy's shirt. He wasn't brave enough to try this with Sandy or Joy, who would've pounded him a good one. Mike would've been thoroughly unimpressed and the threat of payback was too risky. Lucy Rose was a baby at the time. That left Nancy. When the grub's hard legs scrabbled on her lower back, she ran shrieking into the house, where her mother slapped her, either to get her to stop, or because she hadn't taken off her shoes. Nancy couldn't figure out which, and it didn't much matter. It was the definitive moment, the one that proved that her mother hated her and loved the others.

Danny had hired someone to repaint the barns. The pair, standing side-by-side, used to be white, but now they were red. Danny liked tradition and farms simply had to have red barns, even though Dad was responsible for adding these to the farm and they had always been white. Nancy wasn't sure she liked the change. She poked her head into the second barn. Though the cows were out to pasture, she could still feel the presence of their hot, sloppy breath and bulky bodies.

She rounded the far end of the driveway, near the metal equipment shed. The barest of structures, its roof and three rickety sides managed to keep only one out of every ten raindrops off the tractor inside. Danny had plans to replace the shed, now that all the siblings had agreed that he could purchase the farm. Mike had waffled on this point, thinking they could get more for the land if they subdivided it and sold it off in pieces to developers. The sisters backed Danny, who'd been renting the barns and pasture from Mom and had kept the place from falling into ruin. Overruled five-to-one, Mike admitted it was probably better to keep the farm in the family.

Leaving the driveway, Nancy slipped between the shed and calving pens, veering toward what they liked to call the back forty, the northeastern corner of the property. The true back forty was the acreage in the southeastern corner of the farm, as far as one could get from the house without leaving Spolvero land. There was more for kids to do in the north-eastern corner, which was a tumbled concoction of trees, brush, hillocks, grasses, and a murky, leech-filled stream. In contrast, the southeastern back forty was plowed and planted, and not terribly interesting when anything other than tall cornstalks populated the furrows, which was its condition most years.

Nancy worked her way through the high grass and

spindly bushes that preceded the low tree line. The path she and her siblings had worn down to the dirt was scarcely discernible, having been overtaken by plant material. She followed it as best she could until she reached the stream. She sought her spot, a hidey-hole between two hillocks along the bank, and found it with a bloodhound's ease. How often she had spent her tear-filled childhood disappointments here, she could not count. In order to reach the spot, she had to round a hillock, entering the stream bed to do so. The parched year allowed her shoes to remain dry as she clambered up to the natural shelf tucked into the bank, where she took a snug seat and watched the water trickle by. She couldn't believe the others hadn't discovered this place. Sandy and Joy were always sticking their noses into her business, tattling on her just to see her get in trouble with Mom. When she had wanted to be alone here, she had to make sure they weren't snooping after her. Apparently her efforts had been successful, because they never found her here. Mike and Danny had investigated every millimeter of the farm. They must have known, yet, they too had never happened upon her or mentioned the spot. Lucy Rose, well, she was Lucy Rose. Being nine years Nancy's junior, she had been easy to bully. Nancy could give her a loud, "Scat," and an evil look and Lucy Rose would run crying to Mom and Mom would cuddle her and give her whatever she asked for in order to make her feel better.

Looking back, she knew she hadn't been kind to her younger sister, but she'd felt justified at the time, like she'd been balancing an equation. There was the time she had taken Lucy Rose's ring, a ring made from the curlicued handle of a spoon, which Nancy had thought was both crazy and cool at the same time. It was her mother's ring, handed down from her grandmother. Oh, how she had wanted that ring, and her mother knew it. Instead, Mom gave it to Lucy Rose. Nancy's neck and shoulder muscles balled into gristle at the injustice, which felt as fresh today as it had back then.

After swiping the spoon ring off Lucy Rose's dresser,

Nancy had high-tailed it out to this spot by the stream in order to try it on. It fit her forefinger to perfection, twisting delicately up and around, not quite reaching her knuckle. The ring was much too big for her little sister and she probably wouldn't wear it anyway. The childish rationalization allowed Nancy to keep the ring, even though she'd never be able to wear it in the presence of her family. The stolen ring was surely grounds for one of Dad's belt lickings, but it was the prospect of Mom's hairbrush and tongue-lashing that held the secret fast.

She had kept the ring here, between the hillocks, in the pocket of an exposed root, and she searched for it now. Her knees pushed into the dirt of the nook's seat as her fingers sought the cranny along the backside of a particularly large and knobby root.

"Whatcha looking for?"

At the sound of the voice overhead, Nancy scraped her knuckles and lunged forward, almost hitting her head on the bank. Instantly, she was a skulking fifteen again. "Nothing," she replied to the disembodied question.

"It's not there, in case you're wondering."

"What's not here?" Nancy stood in the nook, her position giving her a clear view of her brother's feet.

"The ring."

"What ring?" She wiped dirt from the knees of her jeans, trying to adopt a tone of nonchalance.

"Lucy Rose's ring. You know the one."

"Let me think . . . ." She wondered why she remained on the defensive with Danny about something that had happened when they were kids.

"Come off it, Nancy. The spoon ring. We all know you took it."

Truth, meet fresh air, she thought. A vague relief overcame her. "You did? How?" she said.

Danny laughed and said, "You're lousy at keeping secrets."

"Who knew?" She scratched the tip of her nose with the

side of her finger. "Did you tell Mom and Dad?"

"Nah. Here, give me your hand." Danny helped his sister up out of the nook. "We couldn't do that to you. It'd be like sending you to the lions."

"If they didn't know, who did?"

"The rest of us, though I think Dad suspected."

"Even Lucy Rose?"

"Yeah, even her. C'mon, let's walk back to the house. We've got work to do."

They wended their way back through the scrub, following the path they had cut.

"Why didn't she say anything?" said Nancy.

"I bribed her."

"You didn't. With what?"

"DQ. I promised her three Blizzards, but she managed to get about ten of them out of me before she let it go. Spent most of what I earned in a month cleaning the butcher shop."

"Was that what you were doing with Dad? I knew you went to work with him, but somehow I pictured you cutting meat like he did."

"That was later. He started me out on sweeping the store. That's what I was doing the summer you took the ring. After a while, Dad had me mopping and scrubbing the cutting area. He was one tough inspector. He'd make me do the whole thing over again if ever he found a speck of meat left behind."

"Don't you think that's a good thing?"

"Now I do, but back then . . . ."

They reached the calf pens and looked out over the pasture to a lone tree partially encircled by a pile of rocks on the south side. "Remember the time we found pieces of an old still out in that tree?" Danny said.

"Barely," she replied. "That was a still? It looked like garbage to me."

"Seems the farm was a blind pig during Prohibition."

"Really? They made hooch here?"

"Yeah, heavy-duty operation. It was raided a bunch of times by sheriff's deputies. They never caught the ringleader, a guy by the name of Felix Popp. From what I gather, he was into all kinds of scams. Crooked as the day is long, or so they say."

"How is it you're younger than I am, but you know so much more, kiddo?"

"Maybe it's 'cause I pay more attention." Danny gave his sister a friendly poke in the upper arm.

Nancy poked him right back. "Maybe it's 'cause you're nosy."

"Maybe. Say, the house isn't gonna clean itself. We'd better get to work."

They headed back to the house, pausing at Nancy's minivan. "You want to give me a hand with these supplies, Danny? I got the Greased Lightning you wanted. I still think you're nuts for suggesting it."

"Just you wait, Nancy-girl. You're in for a treat."

They entered through what they called the back door, even though it was technically on the side of the house. As they came into the mudroom, Nancy let out a low half-whistle. "What happened in here?" Brown paper grocery bags filled with empty tin cans, glass jars, plastic bottles, old newspapers and magazines were stacked three and four deep and two high around the perimeter of the small room. Some of the upper bags threatened to topple. Straight ahead in the laundry room, Nancy saw more grocery bags amid mounds of clothing.

"You haven't seen the half of it. That's just the recycling Mom couldn't bear to part with."

"What the . . . . Why didn't you take it to the landfill?"

"She wouldn't let me touch it. I tried to sneak a few bags out once toward the end, but she kept count and wouldn't let me back in the house after that."

"She wouldn't let you in?" There was hardly room to walk in the mudroom. With bags of cleaning supplies dangling from her arms, Nancy tried to push a section of the recycling pile back toward the wall with her foot. A dangerous sound arose as glass shifted.

"Careful, there," said Danny. "Yeah, that last few months. She'd meet me at the door and stand there while I talked to her. I told you she was getting paranoid, but you wouldn't listen."

"Mom's always been paranoid. How was I to know she was getting seriously paranoid?"

"The word 'psycho' should've tipped you off." Danny swung the bags he was carrying, gesturing toward the interior. "C'mon into the kitchen. Let's see if we can find a place to drop this stuff."

The counters were piled with dishes sorted into stacks and groupings by type; small plates on top of big plates, cereal bowls nesting in mixing bowls, coffee cups in a section, with drinking glasses being neighborly. Pots and frying pans were stacked awkwardly upon baking pans and each other. Utensils soaked together in a roaster of semi-soapy water on the floor.

"What have you been doing, Danny? Eating for twenty?"

"This isn't my mess. Set your bags on the floor, wherever you can find a spot. I'll clean out one of these sinks . . . ." He reached into a slurry of greasy, gray water and pulled the drain plug. "You should've seen it before. It's almost livable, now."

Nancy felt the grit of sand and food particles under the soles of her shoes as she walked across the kitchen floor and deposited her bags at the base of the stove. "You call this livable? It ought to be condemned."

"Hey, it's not that bad. The only place I found mouse droppings was in the cupboard where Mom kept the chips and crackers."

"How nice." She went around the L-shaped counter to the dining area. The table was awash in shopping fliers and clipped coupons. All but one of the chairs was missing. Mom's seat at the head of the table remained. This was where Danny had found her. Nancy tucked that picture to the back of her thoughts. "Is the whole house like this?"

"Pretty much. Check out the living room."

A child's tea party gone awry awaited Nancy in the living room. As she entered the dim room, she could make out dozens of lumpy silhouettes. The curtains were drawn, giving the north-facing room an atmosphere of dusk, even though the daylight was full outside. Nancy flicked a switch, illuminating two end table lamps and a floor lamp. The dining room chairs were here, mixed in with the couch, living room chairs and loveseat. The furniture was arranged in a roughly circular manner, with teddy bears and baby dolls occupying every millimeter. Those that didn't fit on the furniture sat at attention on the floor. All eyes were trained in glistening paralysis on an empty office chair in the center of the room. The hairs on Nancy's neck rose, prickling as if a box elder bug had suddenly hitched a ride. She wiped the feeling away and refocused, concentrating on the perimeter of the room instead of the middle.

She noted that the television had been removed from the entertainment center. It had been replaced with a collection of snow globes, which reinforced the impression of a room full of eyeballs, only these had floaters. What had been the Spolvero family library, a high bookshelf along the wall between the two living room doors, appeared at first glance to have been cleared of its books. Smaller bears and babies crowded the shelves. Nancy imagined them jostling for a good view of the performance.

She studied the collection, marveling at the variety. She squatted to see the lower shelves. On the bottom one, she discovered a small selection of children's books underneath a familiar stuffed, yellow-brown bear with tattered ears. She picked him up and rubbed his left ear against her right cheek. It was Honey-B, her bear; the one Mom had snatched away right before Nancy started school. Mom had said that big girls didn't need silly toys and now that Nancy was going to school, she was, by definition, a big girl. Nancy had pleaded with her mom to let her keep Honey-B. She promised she would leave him in her room and not carry him around anymore. She cried. She bargained, saying that she would do anything, anything her mother asked, if only she could keep Honey-B. She cried more and threw a tantrum. She kept up her campaign for a week, until Mom broke a hairbrush on her backside.

Her biggest regret where Honey-B was concerned was that she hadn't been able to give him a proper goodbye. She sat cross-legged. Her eyes teared up as she said, "Hi, old friend. Where've you been?" She rubbed his right ear against her left cheek and laid him gently in the crook of one of her legs.

The books upon which Honey-B had been sitting were as familiar as the bear himself. Nancy shuffled through them, finding Dr. Seuss's *Oh Say Can You Say?* and Jack Kent's *Little Peep*, along with three Little Golden Books: *The Saggy Baggy Elephant*, *The Poky Little Puppy*, and *Doctor Dan the Bandage Man*. These had been her favorite books. What were they doing here? And why weren't any of her brothers' or sisters' books on the shelf? By rights, Lucy Rose's *Curious George* collection should be here. Mom was forever reading the naughty monkey stories to Lucy Rose. Come to think, Mom had never read much of anything to Nancy, certainly not the books she had in hand. This onerous task was left to her older siblings, or to Dad, if he wasn't too tired after work at the butcher shop and farm chores.

She sighed and got up, taking Honey-B and the books back to the kitchen. Danny was sloshing around in the sink, elbow deep in fresh suds.

"Freaky, isn't it?" he said.

"You're not kidding. It's like a horror movie, or something. I kept expecting someone in a mask to jump out at me with a knife."

Danny laughed.

"What got into Mom?" said Nancy. "If we left toys in the living room, she had a fit."

"She began collecting stuff after Dad died. Once she got going, she couldn't seem to stop – something you would've known if you'd ever bothered to visit."

"Don't start, Danny. You know she couldn't stand me. I was giving her what she wanted."

"That's what you think."

"No, that's what I know. Say, mind if I keep these?" She held up the bear and books to show her brother.

"Isn't that Honey-B? I thought Mom got rid of him," said Danny.

"How do you remember Honey-B? You were what . . . three at the time?"

"You carried on so, who could forget? Where'd you find him?"

"On a shelf in the living room. These books belonged to me, too."

"See anything of mine?"

"If I did, I wouldn't recognize it."

"Figures," said Danny. He pulled a frying pan he'd been scrubbing out of the sink and inspected it. "Darn, this thing is impossible to clean. Did you get any baking soda?"

"No. It wasn't on the list. How 'bout that Greased Lightning?" she said with a smirk.

"You're so dramatic, Nancy. All I need is an abrasive . . . ."

"What do you mean, I'm dramatic? There's Comet in one of the bags."

"Nothing. That'll do."

"So, can I keep these?" Nancy waggled Honey-B at her brother.

"Sure, they're yours, aren't they? I've got no use for them." He shook his hands, spraying droplets on the floor, and dug through the bags of cleaning supplies until he found the Comet. He straightened and said, "Am I the only one who's going to do anything around here today?"

"Poor Danny. You're such a martyr. I said I'd help and I'm here, so give me something to do." She set Honey-B and her books on a sheaf of coupon fliers on the table. "Where should I start?"

"Why don't you tackle the downstairs bathroom? I saw you got rubber gloves. You'll be needing those. You'll also want to fill and empty your bucket in this sink. The plumbing is not good in there. Throw some drain cleaner down the tub and sink before you do anything else. That'll give it some time to work. I think I managed to unclog the toilet, but you may want to check it to be sure."

"Got it." Nancy picked up a bucket and Danny grabbed it away from her.

"Here, I'll fill this for you while you take what you need into the bathroom."

"Thanks." After rummaging around, she selected some supplies and headed for the bathroom, which was accessed through the office, only the office was no longer an office. It had been turned into a bedroom. A single bed with a crumpled, faded quilt was crammed against the far wall. The pillow retained an indentation, as though someone had suddenly been called away from a nap. Next to the bed was a small, square mahogany table, serving as a nightstand. And, there, on top, was Lucy Rose's *Curious George* anthology.

Of course, thought Nancy.

The collection of bears and babies continued on the dresser, with little bottoms sitting daintily on a crocheted dresser scarf. The cloudy mirror behind the collection reflected a multitude of backs and a wistful woman in rubber gloves trying to hang onto the accoutrements of tidiness.

As Nancy stepped into the bathroom, her nostrils flared with the acrid odor of old urine. There was a stickiness underfoot. She turned on the light switch with an elbow and was greeted with an unholy sight. This was not her mother's bathroom. Her foot had found a trail of yellow, solidified in mid-stroll from a pool by the toilet. "Eyew!" she said. She backed up into the bedroom. She wasn't going to set her supplies on that floor. Instead, she arranged them on the bedroom floor, just outside the door.

Danny brought in a bucket of fresh, steamy water and made a swift exit, calling out, "Good luck," over his shoulder.

Nancy shouted, "Chicken!" back and mumbled, "Sure, give me the worst job in the house."

While gingerly avoiding the pee, she took inventory, deciding where to start. The lid and seat were up on the toilet, undoubtedly as a result of Danny's efforts to unclog it. Who'd want to look at it otherwise? The inside of the bowl was covered in a patchy orange film, mottled with black spots. The rim was a mess of brown urine and pubic hair. A cup's worth of water resided in the hole in the bottom of the stool, not enough to make a plunger effective. She flipped the seat and lid down. She'd tackle the toilet later.

Top down. That's what Mom always said about cleaning. And she would know. She had been the High Priestess of Cleanliness. Nancy's friends had another name for her: Mrs. Spiffy Spotless. Nancy blushed in recollection. When she was fifteen, she'd been allowed to have a birthday party that included more than her family. She invited several friends, who picked up on her mother's incessant tidiness: The starched apron and dust cloth, the hermetically sealed living room furniture covered in plastic, the high-pitched nag to "Keep it neat in there, girls!" There was the indignity of Mom forcing her friends to change into fresh bootie socks when they entered the house. Savoring the cake, chocolate with white frosting (no sprinkles allowed because they were too messy) had been impossible. Mom kept the vacuum wand at the ready while they ate, practically sucking the chocolate crumbs right out of their mouths. Until this episode, Nancy hadn't realized that her mother was out of the ordinary. The observations and, if she was being honest with herself, the tittering of her friends, had given her a new perspective. Her mother was Mrs. Spiffy Spotless, an object of disdain. Her friends didn't let her forget it, either. When they were feeling particularly snotty, they'd chant "Mrs. Spiffy Spotless" at her until she was on the verge of tears.

When she looked at the situation now, Nancy realized that her mother had been suffering from obsessive/compulsive disorder. Having a name for it didn't make it hurt any less. Mom had dragged them all into her neatness fetish, making them live by her rules, even Dad, and was unrelenting if things didn't meet her specifications. Bedroom baseboards. That was the worst. If Nancy skipped dusting the baseboards in her bedroom during a routine cleaning, Mom would call her on it and make her go around the room twice on hands and knees while she watched. Nancy took to feeling sorry for dust motes. They were doomed. Surely, they had quavered as much as she had in Mom's presence.

But, the dust motes won in the end. When had her mother decided that the war on filth couldn't be won and had simply stopped trying? After Dad died, like Danny said? Was that it?

She brought her mind back to the task at hand. Start at the top and work your way down. Other than the ceiling and walls, the highest surfaces in the bathroom were the mirror and shower curtain. The mirror was dotted with toothpaste spittle. The shower curtain was pulled across the tub, the mold on it indicating that what was behind was probably just as unpleasant. How could her mother have allowed things to get this bad? Could OCD go away?

The mirror was an easy fix. A few spritzes of glass cleaner and a couple of paper towels gave Nancy a feeling of accomplishment. She yanked the plastic shower curtain off its rings, not caring whether she ripped it. It wasn't going to be saved. As she crunched it into a misshapen ball, she checked out the condition of the tub. A ring of black encircled its midpoint, a stubborn girdle. The bottom had a yellowish cast. It couldn't be, could it? More pee? She'd been half holding her breath, trying not to inhale the bathroom odors too deeply, lest she gag. She lowered her nose to tub level and took a tentative whiff. Her throat muscles went into spasm. She swallowed hard and ran to the door, tossing the wadded shower curtain into the bedroom and panting for a neutral smell.

"Right then. No more breathing," she told herself. She put on a skimpy paper face mask, more as a reminder than as an actual odor barrier, and marched back to the tub with the bucket of hot water. "Screw top down cleaning," she said and she tossed the water into the tub to wash down the pee. The water sloshed and settled, diluting the urine, but not taking it away. She had forgotten the clogged drain. The water wasn't completely immovable. If she watched closely, she could make out a miniscule amount of seepage, which unsettled her in a way that full stagnancy couldn't match. Her chest felt strung with rubber bands pulled into the desperation of potential. She wanted to stamp her feet, to will the water to speed up and go down the drain. Instead, she reached for the plunger and worked it with all her might, forcing it into a hard kiss with the drain. Splatter was the payback. Incensed, she attacked the drain again, plunging over and over without making the appropriate contact, until her arms ached and the face mask slipped to her chin.

"Damn!" She threw the bucket into the tub.

"Problems?" Danny leaned against the door frame, a half-smile dancing across his lips.

"It's this goddamn tub. It's plugged and full of pee." She swept strands of hair back from her forehead. They had come loose from her ponytail. "Why was Mom peeing in the tub?" It was more of a demand than a question.

"Why are you blaming me? I have no idea." As an afterthought, he added softly, "And I try not to think about it."

"I'm not blaming you. It's bad enough having to come in here and see everything a mess, but pee in the tub? Pee on the floor? Mom would have sooner died before living like this." Nancy waved around a scolding forefinger, not knowing exactly where to point it. "Is she trying to torture me from beyond the grave? Is that it? She can't resist getting in one more dig, can she?"

Danny looked down at his hands and twined his fingers together. "In case you hadn't noticed, Mom did die, rather than live like this."

"She has always done her best to make me miserable. And still she isn't finished with me. I did nothing but clean this house growing up and now that I'm an adult, I'm still cleaning her house. She's hanging over me . . . I just know it . . . she's got that awful powder blue hairbrush and she's waiting for me to screw up so she can whack me with it."

"Why are you making this all about you?"

"All about me? What? So now I'm supposed to feel guilty for being mad at a dead woman? She was an insane harpy and I'm glad she's . . . ."

"Don't say it," said Danny. He was bristling in the doorway, looking ready to charge. "You think you're the only one who's had a difficult life? Well, boohoo to you. Did you ever stop to think about Mom in all this? What she went through?"

"What she went through, nothing." Nancy was still in full rant, flailing her arms to make her point. "She had a perfect life. Dad adored her and did everything she asked. She never had to work; she had a nice house . . . ."

"I'm talking about her life before Dad." He let the volume of out of his voice and finished with, "When she was a kid." He rubbed his nose and sighed.

The shift in tone grew a cactus of worry in Nancy's gut. She crossed her arms over her chest and said, "What do you mean?"

"Mom was kidnapped when she was eight."

"Excuse me?" She had to have him repeat it, even though the prickling in her stomach signaled that she had heard him correctly.

"She was at Sunday school . . . it was after . . . and she was waiting for Grandpa Bernie to come get her. A guy picked her up instead. Kept her a couple of weeks, then dropped her off at the church again."

"Oh, my God." Nancy sat on the edge of the tub, oblivious to the filth. "Why didn't anyone tell me?" She thought of her own daughters, Lily and Flora. Lily was eight. How would she feel if Lily was suddenly gone?

"Really, besides Grandpa and Grandma and Mom's siblings, only Dad knew. After Mom was returned, she refused to talk about what had happened. Her silence was encouraged because people didn't run off to a psychologist for these sorts of things at the time." Danny pointed to the toilet and said, "Mind if I sit?" With a nod from his sister, he took a seat and continued. "Grandma and Grandpa wouldn't let anyone else mention it in front of her, figuring the memory would fade."

"How did you find out?"

"Dad told me. It was one of the benefits of following him in the business. While we were processing meat, he'd pass on family stories. He swore me to secrecy about this 'til after Mom died. I think it was hard for him to keep it to himself."

"No kidding." An involuntary ripple of nausea went through Nancy as she attempted to absorb the news. "Did they catch the guy?"

"Not that I know of. There was a search when Mom went missing. Practically everyone in Greenville was involved. It was headline news. After Dad gave me the approximate date, I went over to the Watercott Museum and looked it up in the newspaper." Danny ran his fingers through his hair. Nancy noticed that it was starting to thin on top, just like Dad's had done. "It's weird," he said, "to see pages and pages of front page news and to think, if she hadn't been returned, none of us would be here." His voice caught. He cleared it, shook his head and said, "She was just a little kid."

Nancy sat quietly, nursing the lump in her throat. There was nothing to say.

Danny patted her knee. "You know, Nancy-girl, Dad always said you reminded him of Mom. She knew it, too. That's why she was so hard on you. It's not that she didn't love you, or that she was trying to play favorites, even though that's how it may have looked at . . . . Hey, now, don't cry." He looked around for a tissue to offer to his sobbing sister. He found a half-roll of toilet paper under the sink that was partially water stained, tore off the ruined section and offered the rest to Nancy.

"You know your special spot by the creek? We kids all knew about it, even Lucy Rose. Want to know why none of us ever bugged you there?"

Nancy nodded behind her wad of damp toilet paper.

"Mom wouldn't let us."

At this, Nancy cried for her mother and for herself and for her mother as a child, shredding the toilet paper with her tears, while her brother looked on.

When she was done, Danny said, "Here, now, I'll help you with those drains. I think we'll have more success if we open the traps, rather than using drain cleaner. You gonna be okay?"

Nancy bobbed her head and blew her nose.

"You still want to help?" he said.

"Yep," came out with conviction. Nancy regrouped her ponytail. She moved deftly from sink to toilet to tub to floor, scrubbing and polishing the gunk and pee out of her mother's bathroom, not minding for once her mother's discarded wet hairs that clung to her fingers and the cleaning rag like anorexic leeches. She worked until the bathroom sparkled. She emptied her final bucketful of gray water into the toilet. It disappeared with a satisfied glunkle down the drain and as it went, Nancy could see what her mother had gained from making one small corner of the world spotless.

r

Story 7
Googers

His name was Leroy James Budsbanowski and he had a thing for shoes. Sleek leather skimmers, jute wedges, alligator pumps, flaming stilettos, open-toed mules. His neighbor, whom he could see bouncing a Super Ball on the sidewalk two stories below his bedroom window, was wearing a fun pair of canvas high-tops. Their bright turquoise background was covered in Jackson Pollack drips and swirls, which were accented with loud orange shoelaces. He wasn't much for tennis shoes, but it would be easier to persuade him to put on a pair if they looked like the ones on his neighbor's feet.

He wasn't sure who to thank for his interest, and being only six, it hadn't yet crossed his mind to contemplate the issue. His dad, Mr. Frank Budsbanowski, was not to blame. Having descended from stout, rough Polish stock, three-quarters of which inhabited his being through and through, Frank had no time for fancies and frills, found them to be a waste of effort, distracting from the practical matters at hand. Practical matters were the only thing at hand in Frank's world.

Leroy had inherited his father's stubbornness, or so his mother had told him on several occasions. He was, just this moment, grounded to his room for the umpteenth time in a month for refusing to wear the new skate shoes – black nappy leather with red piping – that his parents had bought him. His father insisted that he have stomp-about shoes, something he could get good and dirty in, while Leroy insisted back that he was not a stomp-about, get-dirty kind of kid. And he wasn't. For a young lad, he had an immaculate room and physical polish that were unnatural, something he heard plenty from his father, but not directly.

"By God, Stella," Frank would say to Leroy's mother, "It's unnatural. Why doesn't he leave his toys all over the place like I did when I was a kid? He never plays in the dirt, never gets grass stains on his knees. Christsakes, Julie gets dirtier than he does. I remember Mom forever getting on me about blowing holes in my pants." Stella would reply with, "And if he did that, darling, you'd be all over him about the cost of clothes, wouldn't you?" That sort of logic usually reduced Frank to a low grumble.

It was the word 'unnatural' that stuck with Leroy, though he couldn't say exactly why the word bothered him. What was unnatural in his opinion was the scale of the skate shoes in proportion to his body. He had tried them on again and again and stood in front of his full-length mirror trying very hard to like them so that he didn't have to be grounded, but it was no use. The clunkers made him look as though he had giant puppy paws, rather than accentuating his whippet-like body. The only saving grace of the shoes was that they complimented his hair color, which wasn't exactly black, but was dark enough to read as black in the proper light.

It was decided. He wasn't going to wear them again. Dad could ground him for a string of Saturdays, but it wouldn't make him any fonder of the skate shoes. He stood at the window in his stocking feet and vaguely watched the leaves and tree branches gently bob on the wind. He wished he could go outside and talk to his neighbor, who was gearing up for a walk. Instead, he traced a glittering silver star sticker that he'd affixed to the sill in order to dress it up. Dad hadn't liked that either, complaining about how the house would lose value. Whatever that meant.

Leroy sighed and returned to the skate shoe dilemma. The offensive things sat on the floor at the end of the bed. He was tired of looking at them. He took them to the closet, where he arranged them in such a way that there was distance between them and his other shoes. He didn't want them contaminating the others, which were what Dad called dress shoes. Leroy couldn't understand why his Oxfords, one pair brown, one pair black, were considered dress shoes. Businessmen wore shoes like these every day, as did his great uncle. His deck shoes, one pair khaki, one pair in varying tints of olive green, were classified as casual, as were his deep cherry penny loafers. He had explained this to his father, who pointed out that other boys didn't wear loafers and deck shoes to school, and certainly not Oxfords. When Leroy tried to argue that Julie was allowed to wear slingback sandals to school, which were dressier than deck shoes, his father had said, "That's different. She's a girl." Upon asking, "Why is it different for girls?" his father had said, "End of discussion. You're grounded. Get up to your room and don't come down until those tennis shoes are on your feet."

He looked again at his Oxfords and called his great uncle to mind. The man was Leroy's namesake at his mother's insistence. She got naming rights on Leroy because Dad had gotten to pick Julie's name. He, the man for whom Leroy was named, was Leroy's mother's father's brother, a relationship that most six-year-olds might not keep straight, but wasn't a problem for Leroy. He'd already had to contend with spelling Budsbanowski, which was the longest last name in his kindergarten class. Dad hadn't liked that Mom wanted to name Leroy after his great uncle and lobbied to have him called Frank, Jr., saying, "No son of mine is going to be named after a bum," to which his mother had responded, "You do know, Frank, that Leroy means 'the king' in French, don't you? Besides, Leroy is retired and free to do as he pleases." That was the family story he'd heard, anyways.

Regardless of how his father felt about his great uncle,

Leroy liked the old man and envied his unscheduled, unregimented existence. He didn't get grounded for wearing the shoes he wanted to wear. Normally, Leroy couldn't abide by mismatched shoes – they were as disruptive to his psyche as the oversized skate shoes – but he gave his great uncle a permanent exemption to the rule. The pairing of a black Oxford with a brown one suited his great uncle's lifestyle of crumpled comfort. The overall effect pleased Leroy's sense of equilibrium. The look was consistent with the personality underneath, which Leroy instinctively knew was the ultimate point of clothing, even if he couldn't quite have articulated as much.

When he was satisfied with the placement of the skate shoes, heels aligned with a thin grout line in the tile, toes pointed out, Leroy closed the closet door, listening for it to latch. If it didn't catch correctly, it would swing open, allowing full view of what was inside. He wasn't about to let people nose around looking at his clothing hanging from hangers. Clothing didn't look right that way, all limp and shapeless. His clothes were well-ordered – pants with pants, shirts with shirts, color-coordinated to such tidy degree that it would make Martha Stewart proud. Leroy wouldn't have it any other way, but even so, there was a saying about not airing dirty laundry that he took to heart. Dirty or clean, laundry was laundry and it simply wasn't meant to be seen until it was being worn.

Leroy sat cross-legged on the bed and considered his options. He was so used to being grounded that he'd developed an inventory of activities to keep himself occupied until his mother came to get him. Dad was the grounder, Mom was the ungrounder. She'd leave him in his room long enough to satisfy Dad and then, if time permitted, she'd take him out of the house on errands. While on these after-grounding excursions, she'd say to him, "Your father is all bluster, dear. Eventually he comes around, but it's best to let him think he's having his way for a while. Just think of his yelling as a giant windstorm that has to blow itself out." If

Leroy was feeling particularly sad about one of Dad's wind-storms, Mom would buy him a little something . . . a book, a puzzle, stickers, a drawing pad and colored pencils, a stuffed animal . . . a little something he could use the next time he was grounded.

Today, none of these possibilities seemed exciting. Instead, Leroy was thinking about sneaking into his sister's room, which was separated from his room by a shared bathroom. Julie was almost never in her bedroom during the day, so there wasn't much risk of being caught.

His spine went rigid and he cocked his ear, listening for sounds of activity on the second floor. Hearing none, he slid off the bed and went to the bathroom door. He listened at it for a moment and, being met with silence, slowly opened it and skated across the cream and gold linoleum in his stockings. Upon reaching the door to Julie's room, he performed the same reconnaissance exercise and when he felt that all was clear, he entered.

His eyes shifted about the room. He had a specific mission: Locate Julie's Mary Janes. Miscellaneous Bratz dolls, grooming supplies, makeup, shoes, and clothing were clumped about the floor, reminding Leroy of the midden piles of squirrels. They made his search more difficult, but not unexpected. Julie was a first-class pig. Unfortunately, she was an observant pig. If he moved anything, even an object as small as a barrette, she would know and tell on him. This didn't deter him. The Mary Janes were worth another grounding.

He found them under the bed. They were cockeyed; one was even on its side. Obviously, she had thrown them here. *She doesn't deserve shoes as fine as these*, he thought. She called them googers, which always sounded like boogers to Leroy. It was exasperating, that's what, not getting the name right and calling them something gross. He pulled them out, one at a time, handling them the way his mother handled the Ukrainian egg she had gotten from a friend. The black patent leather was scuffed at the toes. Not wanting to use his shirt, he polished them with Julie's fluffy comforter. He straightened the twisted straps, which were wearing through at his sister's tightening point. She needn't yank them the way she did, but she didn't care. They were merely another replaceable pair of shoes to her. As soon as she outgrew them, they'd be gone, given to Goodwill, or, at the rate the straps were going, out in the trash.

He settled his feet into the Mary Janes, threading the straps through the buckles, poking the tine on each into a hole beyond the one his sister used. He looked at his feet and smiled. They were big, but not too big. Not skate shoe big at any rate. He floated over to the full-length mirror. The shoes were him; they captured his essence the way that one black and one brown Oxford summarized his great uncle's soul. He reveled in being whole with only God as his witness, pirouetting to get a view of the Mary Janes from all sides.

"What the hell are you doing in Julie's room?"

The windstorm had entered without Leroy hearing the hint of a gust. The pleasure of true being disappeared in fright. The boy's heart quivered in a staccato beat as he swung around to face his father.

"Are those her shoes on your feet?"

Leroy stuck out his chin, bracing himself for the on-slaught, and nodded.

"Take them off now. I'm not raising a goddamn sissy."

"But, Dad, why are these sissy shoes? Is it because my sister wears them?"

"Don't get smart with me, boy. You're already ground-ed."

"I'm not getting smart, Dad . . . really." Leroy looked at his feet and picked at his fingers. "I like these shoes and I want to wear them."

"Over my dead body you will," said Frank, who seemed to double in size with the statement. "You're going to take them off and put on your new tennis shoes and you're going to like them."

"Christopher Robin wears Mary Janes," Leroy said softly, adding, "And no one thinks he's a sissy."

"Who in God's name is Christopher Robin?"

"You know, from *Winnie the Pooh*."

"Why am I having this discussion? Who cares about Christopher Robin? This is the real world and in the real world, boys don't wear girl shoes." Frank grabbed Leroy by the elbow, pinching hard on the nerves, causing him to yelp. "If I have to, I'm going to staple those tennis shoes to your feet." He dragged him toward his bedroom.

Panic overtook Leroy. "Please, don't make me wear them! Can't I wear my deck shoes?" The pitch of his voice rose. "Please, oh, please. I don't want to wear them."

His knees locked, making it more difficult for his father to move him. Frank pulled harder, lifting as he did so. Leroy could feel the loose Mary Janes leaving his feet. He stumbled on them as his father yanked him through the bathroom and into his bedroom.

"Frank, what do you think you're doing? Get your hands off that boy right this minute!" Stella's greeting came with a glower. Her hands resided firmly on her hips. Leroy had the impression that she was forcing them to stay there in order to keep from hitting something. She wasn't looking at him, but at his father. Frank dropped him and he tumbled to the floor.

"It's time for a little chat, Frank. Go sit yourself down on the bed."

Frank did as he was told. When Leroy was older, he would pinpoint this as the moment his perception of Frank and Stella's relationship had changed. Until now, he had always thought that Dad was in charge, but in this instant, he became aware of the power of Mom.

The next question out of his mother's mouth surprised Leroy as much as it did his father.

"Do you love your son, Frank?"

Leroy's dad cast his eyes toward his lap. He picked at his fingers while Stella continued.

"Because, if you do, the way you're treating him is not about love. And if you don't, we've got a bigger problem."

Frank mumbled a response into his lap.

"Look at your son and speak up. He has a right to know whether you love him or not."

Eyes afire with guilt and humiliation, Frank glared at Leroy. "Of course I do," he snapped.

"How's he supposed to believe you when you say it like that?"

"Say it like what?"

"Don't play stupid, you old grump."

"I'm not old . . . ."

"So, you admit you're a grump, then?"

They were talking over him, about him and through him, as though he was a floral arrangement in the center of a dining table. If he crawled into the bathroom, would they even notice? He inched a hand in that direction.

"Leroy, dear . . . ."

Yep, they noticed.

"Why do you want to wear your sister's googers?"

He cringed at the word and corrected his mother. "You mean her Mary Janes?"

"Yes, her Mary Janes. Why do you want to wear them?"

He thought for a moment, wishing he could say everything he wanted to say about the Mary Janes, but he didn't have the words. He settled on, "They're pretty . . . and they make me happy."

"See, Frank? Don't you want Leroy to be happy?"

"Sure, but couldn't he be happy with something other than girl shoes?" He didn't spit out girl shoes this time, simply said it as though he was puzzled.

"Do you know how much women pay for shoes, Frank? Ferragamos, Prada, Marc Jacobs . . . some of them go for hundreds of dollars a pair. A lot of them are designed by men. Not women, Frank, men."

A glimmer of excitement welled inside Leroy, akin to how he felt when wearing the Mary Janes. Other men were interested in girl shoes, which meant that he wasn't a sissy after all. He drew his knees up to his chest and wrapped his arms around his shins in an effort to contain himself.

His mother continued appealing to his father's practical nature. "You know, if we play this right, we could have a shoe designer on our hands."

He could see his father considering this, the circuits blinking inside his head like the control panel of a cartoon spaceship. "When you put it that way, it doesn't seem so strange. I just don't want people making fun of the boy. And they will if he wears his sister's shoes to school."

"You're right, Frank, he might get picked on, but that doesn't mean he can't have a pair here at home."

"What about the tennis shoes?"

"Forcing him to wear them will make him miserable . . . and you, too, if you think about it. Do you really want to fight with your son all the time?"

"No, but we spent good money on them."

"Good money, what's that? We've wasted more money on other useless junk in this house. What's another twenty bucks? We can give them to Goodwill. Some little boy will be thrilled with them."

"Fine, but he still needs tennis shoes for gym."

"True, but maybe we should let him pick them out, instead of you." His mother laughed and added, "Seems to me that you're the one who wants skate shoes. We could find a pair in your size, if you like. What do you say, Leroy? Should we get your father a skateboard, too?"

Leroy wasn't sure whether he should agree, but his Dad was laughing, too, so he nodded.

His mother squatted, carefully balancing her soft bulk on her tippy-toes. "Come here and give me a hug."

When he did so, he whispered, "Thanks, Mom," into her baby-powder scented neck, where he had buried his face. She whispered back, "Go give your father a hug, too. I think he's feeling left out."

Frank was back to picking his fingers when Leroy approached. He sighed and shook his head slightly as he looked at his son.

"I'm sorry I don't like the skate shoes," said Leroy.

"It's okay." Frank ruffled his son's hair and said, "I do love you, you know."

"I know."   He encircled his father's neck and squeezed hard; his father returned the hug.

"Okay, guys, I've got some errands to run," Stella said. "You want to come with me, Leroy? We can stop at a couple of shoe stores while we're at it."

Not ready to believe that he wouldn't have to wear the skate shoes, he asked, "What should I put on my feet?"

"Whatever you want," his dad said. "If you grab me those tennies, I'll get rid of them for you."

Leroy didn't need to be told twice.

They stopped at the grocery store first. Then it was on to Uncle Leroy's house. En route, Stella explained that she was worried about Uncle Leroy. He was getting confused about things that hadn't confused him before and she feared he wasn't eating right.

"That'll do it, you know," she said. "Older people lose their appetites and then they forget to eat. Malnourishment makes them even more forgetful – not enough vitamins to keep the brain going. If someone doesn't step in and make sure they're fed, they'll starve themselves to death without even knowing it."

Leroy was half listening as they drove through the neighborhoods of Greenville. He was thinking about shoes, specifically the all-too-real possibility that she'd buy him Mary Janes today, and about how often his mother had taken him to shoe stores in the past while they were running errands. During those trips, she'd say, "I have to indulge my shoe fetish, darling. Why don't you have a look around?" Leroy had thought it strange that she rarely bought shoes

on these expeditions; in fact, she almost never tried any
on. With his new perspective, he understood that the trips
had been more for his benefit than hers. He wondered if he
could find a pair of brown Mary Janes, like the ones Christopher Robin wore.

They crossed the old bridge. A light wind riffled the
surface of the Mud River. The sun flecked in Morse code
along the wavelets. Midway over the bridge, a strong flash
streaked through the railing and hit Leroy smack in the eye,
thus announcing their proximity to Uncle Leroy's house.

Leroy didn't question his great uncle's choice of siding,
having grown to think that smashed pop cans affixed to
the outside of a dwelling were a perfectly sensible way of
keeping the elements out. However, he had heard plenty of
others, adults mainly, who doubted his uncle's sanity along
these lines. His mother told him to pay no mind to folks
who spoke poorly of the man, indicating that those likely to
say such things were crazy birds themselves. She didn't like
that people called him the Tin Man. "Technically," she had
said, "Those cans are aluminum, not tin," to which his father
had interjected, "Pop cans used to be made of tin." She had
replied with, "It's just plain rude, not calling him by his
given name because they're too lazy or scared to get to know
him."

Why anyone would be too scared to talk to his uncle,
Leroy couldn't imagine. Maybe it was because he smelled a
little funny, like a musty, musky couch, or perhaps it was because his false teeth clicked when he talked. But these were
things a person could get used to and they barely registered
with Leroy any longer, especially in light of his uncle's other
habits.

Whenever Leroy and his mother came to visit, his uncle
allowed him to help himself to whatever was in the candy
dish, which changed regularly. It could be lemon drops
one day or chocolate mint buttons the next, or jellied orange
slices, or ribbon candy, or peanut butter cups. He was not
limited to one piece and, if his mother hadn't been there, he

was pretty sure his uncle would have let him eat the entire dishful.

If it was warm, like today, they'd share a can of pop, which his uncle called soda. His uncle claimed he couldn't finish a whole one and he'd let Leroy drink from the can after emptying less than half into a coffee mug for himself. When Leroy was done, he got to flatten the can in the can crusher mounted on the wall beside the door and put it on a pile outside for later use. Some of the cans made their way onto the house, but most were recycled for cash.

Aside from the candy and pop, Leroy enjoyed investigating his uncle's many belongings. There was a story to go along with each; all Leroy had to do was ask and his uncle would expound upon the whys and wherefores of the object of choice.

The man lived in what was essentially a one-room cabin, which didn't look as though it could contain all that it did. A small space in the corner of the cabin had been partitioned for a composting toilet using two handmade bookshelves as walls. A flowered bed sheet acted as a door. The bookshelves didn't reach the ceiling and the whole arrangement left Leroy feeling exposed when he had to go. In another corner of the house was a wood stove and between this and the bathroom was a round, café-sized dining table with two chairs. On the other side of the bathroom, along the wall, was the bed. It served as additional seating when the dining chairs and the squeaky, wooden rocking chair were fully occupied, like when Julie came along on visits. Next to the bed was a military footlocker, one that had been issued to his uncle when he had served in the Second Great War. This was where he kept his clothes hidden away, much to Leroy's approval.

There were two meager windows in the house, one above the bed and one above a counter basin that served as a sink. Because there was no indoor plumbing, a hand pump outside supplied water, which was brought in by the bucketful when needed. Leroy's mom said that his great uncle's lifestyle was unusual for this day and age. He'd only gotten electricity three years ago, in the form of two outlets and an overhead light socket, after the fire department learned that he was still using oil lanterns for light. They didn't want him knocking one over and starting a fire.

As sparse as the furnishings were, the house was packed with all sorts of doodads, some of which had been passed down by family members, much of which had been picked up by his uncle on his walks about town. What seemed to Leroy to be hundreds of items, including a hand-operated egg beater, claw hammers and rubber mallets, pots, cast iron frying pans, old saw blades, miscellaneous coffee mugs, fly swatters, heavy, rusted chains, knotted bunches of keys on rings, and a billy club, hung from hooks and nails on the rough horizontal boards that were the interior walls of the house. Anything not hanging was displayed openly on bookshelves – there were two more besides the bathroom ones – or on the shelf that ran the entire circumference of the house near the ceiling. Dozens of baby food jars were filled with screws, washers, sewing needles and pins, nails, paperclips, bolts, buttons, and nuts, plus ones for different denominations of coins. Whatever had been discarded by someone else was not too insignificant for his uncle's collection. When Leroy came over, he helped in sorting recent additions, which earned him either a Kennedy half-dollar or an Eisenhower silver dollar.

Among his uncle's belongings were traps, ranging in size from bear to mouse, that he'd inherited from previous male relatives, including his great-grandfather. Each trap warranted its own set of stories, some from the days before Greenville had become Greenville, when the primary family occupation had been fur trader. Of all the tales his great uncle told, the fur trade stories were his favorite. A sense of high adventure was conveyed about a wild time that had few rules. As his uncle relayed various events, he would pause to explain how each trap worked, how there were clamps that aided in opening the bear trap, for instance, or how a trap had to be attached to the ground so an animal wouldn't drag it off. Leroy could hardly believe that the old man telling him these things knew people who had actually lived in the Way Back When, and had done a fair amount of trapping himself. Each story ended with the same punch line: "Yep, the only traps that get any use nowadays are mouse traps."

Leroy was looking forward to the can of pop and a story when his mother pulled up along the curb in front of his uncle's house. He and his mother alighted on the dirt path that led to the door and went to knock. Hearing no response, which was typical due to his uncle's wandering ways, they entered to leave him a note and instead found the man in bed. He appeared to be sleeping, but was on top of the covers. Leroy knew this wasn't right – his uncle never slept during the day – and his mother's reaction confirmed his apprehension.

"Uncle Leroy," she said as she shook the man. "Uncle Leroy," she said again, louder this time. Getting no response, she felt for the old man's pulse and pulled out her cell phone.

As she waited for someone to pick up on the other end, she said, "I'm sorry, Leroy, but your googers will have to wait."

Story 8

Chris Dickle

Chris Dickle's in a pickle. Chris Dickle was forever in a pickle. What else was new?

Mom would be mad, as she always was. "You're going to be the death of me, Chris," she'd say. That was for certain. Yesterday, it had been over the trench Chris had dug through the rose bushes while playing commando. Today, it would be over the peach pie Mom had left on the counter. It sat there stewing in its own steamy goodness, begging to be tasted.

Fri-day, pie-day, going to have to lie-day.

The pie was for Mom's book club meeting, her one chance to unwind during the month, and she didn't let Chris forget it. No way to lie and say, "I forgot." It started with a flake of crust and proceeded to a toothpick artfully poked into one of the decorative holes in the surface. What good was a flake of crust without a smidgen of gloopy sweet filling? From there, it progressed to a forkful, at which point came the realization that this had gone too far. Mom would notice a missing forkful and go off on her lecture circuit and tweak Chris' ear and follow through with a grounding that was never followed through upon. Mom was too busy to be the enforcer.

Sigh-day, bye-day, why bother to try-day?

Time to get out while the gettin' was good. No sense making Mom go through the lecture and ear tweaking.

Chris left an apology note, being extra sure to enlarge the "I love you" part, even attempting a decorative heart, instead of the preferred blood-pumping and squirting muscular one, and leaving off the usual daggers and ninjas. That ought to do it.

It was time for a walk-about, knock-about, but first a personal inventory was needed.

"Cell phone . . . check!" It was Mom's lifeline, made her feel like she was being a good single mom by keeping tabs on her kid. Chris would be keeping it off until after Mom was due at her meeting.

"Pencils . . . check!" A handful of pencil stubs, no more than an inch long, and some eraser scraps, were essential, just in case there was a chance to draw, to leave a mark.

"Frodo and Han . . . check!" Frodo Baggins and Han Solo action figures, ever at the ready for an epic duel. Frodo had a sword; Han had a laser pistol, which, under normal human circumstances would make for an uneven fight, but Frodo had the ring, so it was all good.

Good battles good battles good battles good. Why did good and evil always have to do battle? It was more interesting to have good battle good because you didn't know who to root for.

"Dice . . . check!" There was the possibility of running into friends and having to settle some dispute. Dice were better than coins in this respect, more nuanced.

"Cash . . . check! Ha!"

Cash or check, cash or check. Cash is better than check. Check, check, check, have a bowl of checkers, but keep a plate for chess.

Eating out was a certainty tonight. Mom would be upset if it wasn't healthy, insisting that Chris try to fit the four food groups into each meal if she wasn't around to cook. She ignored the food pyramid they taught in school, saying it was too complicated. Chris was pretty sure there was room on the food pyramid for an Icee, and there was no law forbidding one for dessert.

A trip to the bathroom . . . fifty cents; tennies firmly tied . . . a quarter; being prepared like a Boy Scout . . . priceless.

With that, Chris was out the door.

A pile of long sticks, appropriate for walking, or as staves or swords, as the situation warranted, was kept in the backyard between the lilac bushes and the shed, the secret stash.

Pick one, stick one, kick one, lick one. Here's a good trick one: Knobby and smooth on one end, making a perfect hand-hold; most of the bark peeled off the length; stout enough to take a solid banging against the neighbor's picket fence. Clacka, clacka, clacka, clacka. Mr. Budsbanowski didn't care for the racket, or the way the stick nicked the paint. Mrs. Budsbanowski didn't seem to mind. It was just a fence to her.

Some days were made for aimless wandering. Today, there was a purpose, a reason greater than simply avoiding Mom's mad. Rumor had it that the Tin Man had moved out of his house. Scottie Scott-meister Hildreth had sent an instant message the previous evening, having heard the news from Garrett the Ferret, who found out from Evan Draggin' Dragoo. Evan thought the other kids were calling him "Dragon." No one had the guts to tell him otherwise. Draggin' got the scoop on the Tin Man from his parents, who were massive busybodies. Chris was convinced they were spies or former FBI agents, because whatever they said usually checked out. It was not a lead to ignore, in any case.

Instant potatoes are better than tomatoes. Step, hop, watch the crack, step, hop, hop again. Give me some p'taters, throw the darn'd t'maters. Whoops, another crack. The sidewalk was bulging, the root of an adjacent tree pushing the cement up enough to create a tripping hazard.

"Thought you could get me, eh? Be gone, thoust Demon of the Dark, who hast invaded thine Tree of Bounteous Life." A couple of jabs with the staff and the demon was beaten back into its Pit of All Despair. A lesser demon didn't take that much effort. Mom wouldn't agree. She said that getting the City of Greenville to fix the sidewalks without charging residents an arm and a leg was like wrestling with a roomful of cranky lesser demons, which would be worse than fighting the Devil himself.

East to the river, passing houses and fences and dogs tied up in yards. They weren't allowed to roam free.

One of the guys, Chad-man McFadden, was out mowing. Upon seeing Chris, he turned off the engine and walked over.

"Hey, man, what's up?"

The requisite handshake: Knuckles together twice, fists pounded top, bottom, top, bottom, a swiping of the palms, finished with forefinger and thumb cocked gun style and a double-click in the cheek.

"Nothing much, Chad-man. Just conducting an investigation. That, and trying to stay out of Mom's hair."

"Oh?" Chad wiped his sweaty hands on his pants.

"Can you blow this joint?"

"Naw. Gotta finish the lawn, then we're gonna visit Grandma at the nursing home."

"Too bad. I'm heading over to the Tin Man's house."

"Your mom lets you go to the east side by yourself? To the Tin Man's house?"

"Hey, what she doesn't know . . . ."

"Mom would kill me if I crossed the river without a grownup. Says it's too far away and I'm too young. Whatever. If I weren't dead meat from that, she'd kill me for sure if I went to the Tin Man's house. She doesn't want me hanging around street crazies."

Chris bristled. "The Tin Man's not a street crazy. What business you got calling him that if you've never met him?"

"Don't get your undies in a bunch, man. It's just what my mom says."

"Huh, what your mom says. You're such a Momma's Boy."

Chad's legs stiffened. He squared and balanced his stance. "Watch it, Dickle. Say another word about Mom and

I'll . . . ."

"You'll what?" Chris moved to shove his shoulder. Chad flinched, even though Chris had controlled the swipe so that contact was no more than a tap of the finger. "That's what I thought."

"Good one. You really had me going there."

"I love messin' with you. It's so easy-peazy lemon-squeezy. No offense about your mom, Chad-man, 'kay?"

"No problem. Sometimes I wish she'd give me more freedom like your mom does."

"Yeah, that'd be cool. Most of the guys are in the same boat. Can't get away because of all the rules and regs. It sucks running around town by myself, especially when I'm on an investigation."

Chad tipped his ball cap back and scratched his scalp. "What are you investigating?"

"I heard the Tin Man's moved out of his house."

"Who's your source?"

"I got it round about, but Draggin' is where it started."

"That dork? Cripes, he knows everything. Probably 'cause he's got nothin' better to do than be snoopy."

"Hey, a guy's gotta have a purpose. Dork that he is, at least he's good at it. I'm heading over to see if it's true."

"Watch yourself. If he's still there and he catches you, you'll be in a world of hurt."

"Naw, I'll be fine. The Tin Man's a good guy. Besides, I'm the Great Dickle. I can talk my way out of anything."

"I gotta get back to work. Good luck. Let me know what happens."

They shared their secret handshake and Chris was off once again.

Spark plugs, milk jugs, ugly mugs, freaky bugs. Squash 'em on the sidewalk, squash 'em on the street, pick 'em up between your toes, just don't squash 'em in your teeth. The staff hit the sidewalk with each step, each step advancing upon the river and the old mill site. A toothy air whistle ushered forth and trailed behind, notes falling and dissipating before hitting the ground.

The mill site, normally a kid's delight with its ruinous walls, mostly decayed water wheel, and buried treasure of square nails and odd coins, failed to keep Chris' attention, even after an attempted death duel between Han Solo and Frodo Baggins and an assessment of the river from atop a half-wall. There would be no lingering today. The investigation – Code Name: Pop Can Quest – was calling. Chris, not knowing what to expect, formulated a plan, or rather, a convenient excuse for being at the Tin Man's house, should the need arise. If the Tin Man was home, there wouldn't be a problem, but, if he wasn't, well, who could tell what might happen? Pop cans would serve the purpose, a reason for being on the old man's property. One wouldn't be enough, but more than four would be too hard to carry. Four it would have to be. An offering, a house warming gift.

Now, to find four pop cans between the mill and the Tin Man's house. Stick swinging and thrashing at the long grass, Chris wended along the river bank, keeping as close to shore as possible without getting wet. "Pop!" And a swing. "Pop!" And a swing. "This shouldn't be too hard." The riverside was a veritable trash heap. "Pop!" And a swing. "Pop cans! Where are you?" Pay dirt. A pile of them – well, a pile of beer cans, anyway - was by the ashy remnants of a fire pit in an area cleared by past revelers. Two cans were smashed and deposited into pants pockets. The other two would have to be carried in the non-stick hand.

Non-stick hand! Just like Teflon!

Walking again. Giggle box, Bono vox, shoes and socks, mental blocks. Approaching the culvert, the fleeting ripple of a thin shadow was spotted in the haphazardly woven grass. Chris dropped the cans and bent to swiftly snatch it up by the tail, although where the tail truly began on the garter snake was anyone's guess.

"Hey, little guy, what's up?" The snake's feathery flicking tongue brushed up, tasting human lips and skin, a first in his short life. All snakes were male in Chris' mind, just like all dogs. All cats, on the other hand, were female, while all goldfish were sexless. Knowing better didn't matter.

Urged by its new human plaything, the snake, who was female and well aware of it, slid up one arm, into the soft cave of a t-shirt sleeve, across a creamy expanse of neck and shoulders, out another sleeve, and down another arm. The snake was a momentary pal. Asking to keep it was a useless pursuit. Mom didn't allow wild things in the house, having dealt with plenty of such experiences when Chris was younger. Whenever the subject was broached, she'd bring up the incident with the crickets. The shoulder-crossing action was repeated several times until it got old, both for the snake and for Chris. A few head caresses later, the reptilian friend was released and the journey, nay, the Quest, resumed.

The culvert was quickly passed. With only the barest trickle of water, it held no romance or adventure.

It was time to play Silent Mental Gross Out, a favorite pastime among the gang, but just as easily played alone. The object of the game was to conjure up the most disgusting thing you could think of in order to see how close you could come to throwing up. When played in a group, one person would be the thinker/barfer, while the others attempted to guess what was making him gag. When played alone, the game was good practice for the eventuality that you might have to fake sick in order to get out of something you didn't want to do. There was nothing like almost barfing to turn Mom to your way of thinking. True vomiting was rarely the result of the game, which typically ended with gut-aching laughter and exclamations of "That's so disgusting!" and "Yuck!" and "Gross!" There was that one time, though. It was when Chad-man had been the thinker. He'd been imagining grape jelly as blood clots, and when he revealed this to the group, Draggin' immediately doubled over and hurled on the ground right in front of everyone. He'd had a grape jelly sandwich for lunch. The sight and smell caused a rapid-fire reaction in the group, with each contributing the contents of his stomach to Draggin's in the game circle. The only exception to the vomitous riot had been Chris, who was known for an iron stomach and had swiftly dispersed the others to fresh air away from the puke. It was a classic incident, one all the guys still talked about.

While the envy of the group, Chris' constitution made it harder to work up the gag reflex. Today's practice, one of many, was an effort to rev it up, to achieve puke on demand, the ultimate control.

Blood spots in raw egg yolks, inhaling sulfurous farts, licking hairy armpit sweat, drinking toilet water, eating boogers and scabs. Nothing. Long, gobby, pale green snot sucking in and out of Draggin's nose. Closer. Touching the warm, mucoid remains of half-chewed cat food that kitty left in a shoe. Swallow hard. Couple that with pulling a thread out of kitty's backside, poop still attached. A sourness in the back of the throat. Swallow again. Stupid kitty. Chewing thread off the spool on the sewing machine. What'd she think was going to happen? Ick! She liked to leave her snot prints in a line all over the windows, too, which took super-strength window cleaner to get off, and she slung spit in a two-foot circumference when she shook her head. Blech! Okay, so it wasn't truly barfable, but poop on a string, that came pretty close.

Rapid progress was made in traversing the river bank to the bridge. Looking up the bank away from the river, Chris could see the Watercott Museum's silhouette looming in the late afternoon sun. During the third grade field trip a few years back, the class had been told the place was haunted, which nearly caused a panic after Draggin' started crying and ran to the front door. He couldn't get it open, which he would later blame on the ghost, but was merely the result of him pushing on the door, rather than pulling to get it open. While the teacher dealt with Draggin', the tour guide tried to back her way out of what she'd just told the students, saying there really wasn't a ghost and they mustn't be afraid. She had looked on the verge of panic herself, but only at the prospect of twenty-five bawling third graders. Chris could spot BS from an adult as easily as bird crap on a black Corvette. So could the rest of the kids, but they were too buffaloed by size, age, and authority to question it. Not so Chris, who said, "Look, lady, if there isn't a ghost, why'd you tell us there was one?" which garnered a sputtered non-reply.

"Don't you think we can handle the truth? My buddy Evan, there, he's a little fragile, but that doesn't mean the rest of us are, does it?" Chris eyed each classmate, nodding and silently bolstering the others until they had the courage to agree. "If there's a ghost, we'll find it, won't we?" More nodding. "All right, everyone, keep on the lookout and listen carefully. We don't want to miss anything. Ready?" With the assent of the others, Chris said to the tour guide, "You may continue; lead the way."

Just as Chris had suspected, there wasn't a single pitiful wail or rattling chain or vaporous apparition experienced on the tour. Likely, the story had been concocted to sell tickets. Even without the ghost, the museum had some pretty cool stuff, and the grounds were worth a good poking around, but not today.

Up a sandy incline to the sidewalk and the bridge was breached. With a sharp crack of the walking stick, Chris declared the bridge, "Mine!" and strode forward with the confidence of a four-star general.

The Dickle Bridge, the Pickle Bridge, the Tickle Bridge, the Nickel Bridge. Chris wished for a nickel from every car now passing over – west to east, east to west – five o'clock rush hour bumped forward an hour because it was Friday.

Fickle nickel, trickle nickel, snickle nickel, chickle nickel. Chickle, chickle, chickle, hmm. A Chiclet would be good about now. The pie had worn off, leaving a belly on the rumble. It would have to wait, chew on its insides a while. The Tin Man's house was calling.

Upon reaching the middle of the bridge, Chris stopped, pulled out a pencil stub, and made a tick mark on a baluster of the intricately scrolled metal rail. It was a ritual of cross-

ing alone. There had to be at least seventy or so ticks since
last summer, when Mom had eased up on her prison guard
protectiveness. The cell phone had been, and still was, the
key to wandering liberty. A pat of the pants pocket in search
of the rounded rectangular bulge affirmed the familial tether,
an electronic leash Chris was glad of, but would not readily
admit.

A boat motor forced a shift in focus over the bridge railing to the water below. The river was in a mood, already
irritated by a gusty wind, now further riled by the churning
wake of a criss-crossing speed boat. Clouds, nowhere to
be seen upon leaving home, were moving in from the west,
jostling each other to be the first to reach the river. They
weren't the happy little clouds of the poufy-haired landscape
painter on public television.

"Rain, rain, go away . . . ." Run! Chris sprinted, cross-
ing the remainder of the bridge in gazelle time, and doubled
over, hands on knees, huffing from the sudden exertion.
"Walk it off." That's what Mrs. Cooley, the phys. ed. teacher,
told students during the track and field unit. "Walk it, walk
it, walk it off . . . walk it, walk it, walk it off." Walking in
circles, round and round, ten times on the manicured grass
beside the sidewalk ought to do it.

Breath cycling down, steadying, muscles no longer
tweaking, mouth moistening, vision leaving the tunnel,
systems powering back to normal. Clouds still there, but
lighter, no longer worrisome, not on this side of the bridge at
any rate. There was time.

The Tin Man's house was dead ahead, a landscaped foot-
path through the city's riverside park ending almost directly
opposite the front door. Yellow police tape was draped between chest-high metal stakes surrounding the house. "Like
that could keep me out."

The park was split by a cobblestone road, which ran
along the north side of the Tin Man's property. It was the
only cobblestone road in town, which led to speculation
among some of the grade schoolers that the Tin Man was

an important guy. Middle schoolers, like Chris, knew better. God bless Draggin'! The City Council was just waiting for the old man to take a permanent dirt nap so they could swoop in and confiscate his land and make it part of the park, which already circled around the east side of the property. The road was one step in the realization of their evil master plan. Oo-oo-wah-ah-ah-ah-ah!

Circle around, look nonchalant, nothing to see here . . . just a kid, whistling and playing with a stick, glancing around once and again at the pop can shack because it would look odd to pretend not to see it at all.

Pop cans! Crap! Somewhere along the way Chris had lost two. There went the excuse should someone come along. Maybe the two left in pants pockets would do. They'd have to. No chance of finding any along this side of the river. The Tin Man was a human metal detector. He kept a good portion of Greenville's east bank picked clean.

Moving closer . . . . There was a no trespassing sign on the door that wasn't there before, and a heavy-duty padlock, twice the size of the one the Tin Man normally used when he intended to be gone longer than an hour or so. Chris knew from previous visits that the key was hidden in a crease of the third aluminum can left of the doorknob so the Tin Man wouldn't forget it. Why the Tin Man trusted Chris with this information was a mystery. Chris imagined it was because the Tin Man recognized a fellow wanderer when he saw one. Wanderers stuck together, had each other's backs.

Scoping fore and aft, no one in sight . . . a dash under the police tape . . . plastering body against the uneven and sporadically sharp wall, hoping to become Super Chameleon and blend into the exposed cabin. The goal was to get a look in one of the windows. Chris chose the less public one on the river side of the cabin, the side on which the Tin Man kept a cyclone fence pen for cans. The pen was empty, an abnormal state. It wouldn't provide any cover should cover be needed. A weathered wooden bench, just long enough for a grown man and a skinny child to share, was beside the pen. It made a good perch for crushing cans with a mallet and now was dragged a few feet and enlisted as a perch for a young spy.

After wiping grime from the window with a bit of t-shirt, Chris peered in and focused on the darkness until it glowed with ambient light. Everything appeared to be as it was during the last visit, but not quite. Scanning with concentration, Chris saw that certain items were missing from the walls: a beaded Ojibwe pouch that had been handed down to the Tin Man by a great-grandmother, a couple of the traps, a box-like basket for keeping caught fish, a pair of shackles from a relative who'd been a slave long, long ago, but who'd been freed by his fur trading master.

The foot locker beside the bed was open and in disarray. Chris hoped whoever had cherry-picked the place hadn't found the Tin Man's Legion of Merit medal. It had been given to him for a particularly daring feat in World War II. He was on a plane with other soldiers, traveling from one island to another – island hopping was what the Tin Man called it – when the pilot was shot. No one else aboard could fly, including the Tin Man, but he grabbed the controls and brought the plane down on its belly in the Pacific Ocean, not too far from their destination. Everyone, with the exception of the pilot, got off the plane uninjured. The story was told the way only the Tin Man could tell it, with a certain heroic detachment, but with all the details in place, like the pilot's name, the number of men on board, and the weather that day. It gave Chris chills.

"Hey, kid! What are you doing?"

Chris about fell off the bench, startled by the sudden harsh voice.

"Get down from there right now, you hear?"

Figures. It was a guy in a city truck. Nosy bugger. "I'm going, I'm going." Chris jumped down and took off toward the back of the house, under the police tape, and headed for the hill with the cemetery.

"Don't you come back. This ain't your property," said

the city worker, who added, "Goddamn kids these days, no respect for nothing."

The investigation, while fruitful, was also disappointing. The Tin Man was gone. Chris wished for one more chat session with the old guy. Speak now, or forever hold your peace. Sleep now, or forever hold your Z's. Poop now, or forever hold your pee.

Chris had to pee. Now. But decent bathroom facilities were nowhere near. No time to find a pot to piss in. A mass of shrubs near the base of the hill would have to do. Chris entered, undoing button and zipper.

How must it be, to stand up and pee, swinging one's dick in the air so free?

Chris squatted, trying not to dribble on her pants as she went.

Twist

It was a funny name. Why couldn't she remember it? Because she has Alzheimer's, dumb ass. Why can't you get that through your thick skull? Lighten up, give Sara a break. And you'd better lose the crabbiness before going over, buddy. She doesn't deserve your bad attitude. It'll just upset her, agitate her to the point of distraction, and the visit will be a waste for both of you. Where the hell is that Smirnoff distributor?

Tom checked his watch. Time was playing tricks on him, making him feel as though it was later than it really was. The distributor wasn't expected for another fifteen, twenty minutes. How to occupy his time? He'd been working at the bar so long that routine tasks could no longer divert his attention. He'd already counted out the change in the till, and then checked it twice to be sure. Or was it three times? Maybe he was coming down with Old Timer's himself. Sara hated that term, Old Timer's. He'd used it once with her, right after she'd been diagnosed and still had her faculties, and she'd slapped him. He'd had it coming. The hard slap of reality. When faced with an inevitable circumstance that was certain to end tragically, he had a tendency to joke, to minimize what couldn't be minimized. He'd been tempted to point out that she always told him she had CRS disease. And now, she really couldn't remember shit. Did she sense that she was slipping, or had she manifested a self-fulfilling prophecy?

He wiped the bar again, though its high polish was unbearable in its reflective perfection. Good thing the late afternoon habitual drunks wouldn't notice or care. They'd have it water-marked and littered with napkins in no time.

There it was – the reminder of time, nagging and nattering. Tom looked at his watch. Five minutes had passed. Inching achingly by. Why had time not gone this slowly during their twenty-five years of blessed togetherness? That time when she knew exactly who he was and behaved as though he was the only man left on earth. He shook his head fiercely, concentrating on the identity crisis and not the other thing. If someone were to walk in at this particular moment, like that Smirnoff distributor, he'd think Tom's bobbling head and muttering were sure signs that he needed to join Sara in the nursing home. That's how seriously Tom was taking his interior monologue. If only he could get her to remember his name.

The back door squealed and banged, throwing a wedge into Tom's spinning mind. Good enough. A reprieve. Maybe something would come to him in the interim.

"Hey-de-ho, Tom!" It was Jake, arriving earlier than expected. Tom couldn't ask for a better employee, though at thirty-three, Jake was still a kid. Heck, he'd always be a kid.

"Howdy, you punched in?" Tom folded the bar rag in half and hung it over the edge of the stainless steel bar sink.

"Not yet. It's a half-hour before I'm scheduled. You want I should do so?"

"Yeah, why don't you. I've got the Smirnoff guy coming in soon, but I want to skedaddle and see Sara before the bar rush."

Jake grabbed a pen and a pad of green order slips and leaned on the bar, pen at the ready. "What do you want me to order?"

"Flavored vodka, a couple cases, assorted flavors, some raspberry, blueberry, lime, cranberry, and green apple. Ever since the Martini Mamas have been coming in, we're going through it like water."

Jake looked up from the order pad and said, "Martini Mamas?"

"You know, that group of ladies that comes in every Tuesday at seven."

"The ones in the khaki pants, white shirts, safari vests and navy blue bandanas?"

"Don't forget the fedoras." Tom picked up the bar rag and resumed polishing.

"Fedoras?"

"Their hats. They take them off when they get here, commandeer a chair or two to set them on."

"Right. You call them Martini Mamas?" Jake chuckled. "I always thought of them as the Safari Sisters."

"When they've got a few in them and they get a little testy, they become the Martini Mafia."

"Good one. Have you noticed that they take over the jukebox, too? If I hear Dido's "Surrender" and Duran Duran's "Hungry Like the Wolf" one more time, I'm going to vomit. Each one has a personal anthem. They play 'em every time they come."

"I wouldn't know anything about that." Tom rubbed one of his substantial white eyebrows. "While you've got that order, check to see if we have enough soda and lemonade. Oh, and limes, too. The ladies like their garnish."

"Got it." Jake wrote then tapped the pen against the pad. "Anything else?"

"Work here long enough and you'll get used to the noise. Won't even hear it after a while. Check our supply of umbrellas. Gotta keep the Mafia happy." Tom refolded the rag and returned it to the sink's edge. "Now go get punched in, boy. I have to get going."

As Tom climbed into his vintage 1951 Chevy pickup, worries about Sara and her shambling memory sprang to the fore, in no small part because she had encouraged the restoration of the truck. He had had it painted red just for her, even though he preferred an unshowy green olive. He couldn't get into the truck without thinking of her. Hell, he couldn't do much of anything without her constant mental presence, although he preferred her constant physical presence. He lived her, their identities irrevocably twined. As her memory failed, he felt himself slipping. If the love of his life couldn't recognize him, what good was he?

It hadn't always been this way, this dependence upon a woman for the ticking of his soul. He'd been a bit of a loner as a kid, mostly because he embarrassed easily, flushing and sweating at the slightest provocation. And provoke the kids did. Cruel little bastards. "Tom Twist made a list . . ." still ricocheted in his ears. Somehow he got by, left primary school not too much the worse for wear, and got married. Sweet Shirley the She-Devil, who delighted in watching him turn a fierce shade of stop light, not from embarrassment, but from unexpressed rage caused by her taunting. She knew his weaknesses and exploited them, jabbing at him forcefully like an inexperienced fisherman filleting a walleye. "Never hit a girl, Tom," his father had instructed when he'd been tempted as a child. And he never did, although he'd been sorely tempted with Shirley. The Seven Year Itch finally put an end to the She-Devil's torture. Not because of an affair on either side of the marital divide, but because of an honest to goodness itch, a full-body rash that Shirley wouldn't go near. As soon as the divorce was final, Tom's hives disappeared.

A couple of years later, he tried again, marrying his second 'S,' Sandra, a petite, perky jewel with glossy midnight hair clipped to chin-length precision. She was perfection, but not for him. He liked a messier life than she did, so they amicably split after a couple of years.

Tom swore off marriage altogether, figuring that the single condition would be his forever. Forever measured in at fourteen years. Well, twelve years and five months give or take, if you counted from the day he and Sara met. Only, it was more of a reintroduction. They had known each other in grade school, but not in a chummy we're-the-same-age way. Sara was younger by four years, which made her too silly and pesky for him to pay her any attention. Her recollection, when she'd been having such recollections, was that he was cute, but dopey and a little stuck-up, and that he never talked to girls anyway, so why bother? This revelation had surprised him, first in that she had been somewhat interested in him all those years ago, enough to notice that he was cute and didn't talk to girls, and second in that he had never felt stuck-up. Apparently this was how others had read his shyness, even though it wasn't what he had intended. Of course, if they hadn't teased him, things might have turned out differently.

Tom negotiated Blue Street east to Eighteenth, waving to those he knew, and rather uncharitably wishing the Tin Man was still on a street corner collecting change. The Chevy had been this route so many times that he almost felt he could take his hands off the steering wheel and the truck would automatically turn right onto Eighteenth, cross Indigo Street, and pull into the parking lot off Violet, coming to a stop at the Rose Hill Rest Home.

It wasn't called a rest home anymore. Rose Hill was now officially called a nursing home, evidence of a shift in God knows whose preference for an active description over a passive one. Tom liked the idea of rest after a lifetime of hard work. Nursing spoke of convalescence and needles and pills and bed pans, rather than shooting the shit and playing cards. He scratched his head over the Rose Hill part of the name, too. The nursing home wasn't on any sort of a hill. Two scrawny, barely-watered rose bushes struggled to reach past the weeds that had overtaken them in front of the Rose Hill sign, a meager attempt by someone to conquer the cognitive dissonance of having no roses at Rose Hill. Tom couldn't recall ever seeing blooms on the bushes.

Cheerful name for a cheerless place, he thought as he pushed the large silver button for the automatic door. He was greeted with a surge of refrigerated air, which lasted while he was in the entryway proper and ended when he got into the main lobby. He subconsciously held his breath for several beats, not wanting to smell industrial disinfectant unsuccessfully masking old bowel movements.

He greeted the receptionist at the front desk and veered left toward a back hall to find Sara's room. Nursing homes had a thing for long hallways. Take the most infirm, least mobile people on the planet and make them travel an interminable distance to piss, or sleep, or eat. It didn't make a whole lot of sense. Good thing the residents had wheelchairs. Sara's room was at the end of one of four hallways, two of which paralleled each other on opposite sides of the building. The trek made Tom wish for his own wheelchair.

A plaintive, regular beeping made itself known as he passed the nurse's station. One of the residents had pushed a call light button for assistance, but there was no staff around the station to hear it and respond. It was appalling. The staff was overworked and underpaid; consequently call lights weren't answered in a timely fashion. Sometimes, depending on who was working, call lights were switched off without being answered at all.

"God damn it, anyway." Tom quickened his pace, hoping it wasn't Sara. He ignored the ache in his left knee and hip. His eyes shifted back and forth, searching rooms with open doors on either side of the hallway for signs of a medical professional. Many of the rooms were empty due to the afternoon activity hour. The few that were occupied held antisocial residents or those who were on such a steep downward grade that they were busy making friends with Death.

Tom found the call light blinking above a doorway two rooms away from Sara's and stuck his head in to monitor the situation. No nurse, but there was Bart Logan, formerly a strapping gorilla of a carpenter, reduced to half his previous size and stranded in a recliner.

"Hey, Bart. You okay?"

Bart shook his head and focused hard, sorting through memories in order to identify the man before him. "Tom?"

Tom nodded and made a noise of encouragement.

"Tom Twist? Twist . . . made a . . . list . . . kissed . . . Twist."

Tom sighed. Not that damn rhyme again. "Yes, Bart, I'm here. Is there something I can get you?"

"Get me?"

Tom spoke slowly and enunciated his next statement. "Bart, you pushed your call button."

"Call button?"

"That button clipped to your chair." Tom moved to the recliner and pointed to the call button. "You pushed your call button. This thing right here. You're supposed to push it when you need something. Do you have to use the bathroom?"

"No, oh, let's see, um, yes."

"You have to use the bathroom? I can find a nurse."

"No, not the bathroom. Um, oh, that's right. That. I can't reach that." Bart weakly gestured toward a bedside table on wheels. It held a plastic bottle of water, a small stack of loose tissues, a cup of applesauce, spoon, and television remote.

"There's a lot of stuff here, Bart. What do you want? Your water? Your applesauce?" He held up each item as he mentioned it.

Bart made a hand gesture, tapping thumb to curled forefinger in an action recognizable to habitual TV viewers. Tom picked up the remote. "This is what you want, isn't it?"

"Yes, that's it. Thanks. What was your name again? Yeah, yeah, um . . . I'll get it . . . ."

"Tom, Tom Twist," he filled in as he rolled the table closer to Bart in case another item was needed.

"That's right. Thank you, Tom Twist."

As Tom turned to leave, a nursing assistant came into the room. "Problem's solved," Tom read her name tag, ". . . Gloria. He just needed the remote."

"I'll make that determination," said Gloria with a pinched look as she switched off the call light. "You may

go." Upon his exit, Tom caught the beginning of her conversation with Bart. "Called me all the way down here for
a remote, did you Bart? What sort of fool thing is that to
do? Don't you know I'm busy?" Tom wished her a future
in a nursing home with a caregiver of her temperament as
he limped off to Sara's room. His hip was demanding a soft
chair.

Strange. A peek into Sara's room garnered her room-
mate, Helga, but not Sara. Where could she be? Normally
she was here during activity hour, being one of the antisocial
ones. Upon catching sight of Tom, Helga shrieked, "Help!
Oh, somebody please help me!" for no apparent reason and
then repeated herself. She was ninety-seven and stone deaf.
There was no way to console her. She always believed she
was in mortal danger, especially when Tom was around.
"Help! Oh, help! Help me!" She'd keep this up until Ruby
or Eileen came. They were the only ones on staff who could
get her to stop. Tom didn't know how Sara put up with
Helga. A single day of this would make him bat shit crazy.

He left without a word, making his way back down
the hallway. Residents were trickling around the building,
scooting themselves in wheelchairs, hobbling with walkers,
and shuffling along the walls, hands on extended lengths of
railing to keep their balance. Activity hour was apparently
over. Tom greeted those he knew, with the realization that
more familiar faces were making an appearance with every
visit. While the physical deterioration of his contemporaries
was sad, and he certainly had no intention of winding up
here, there was comfort in recognition and shared history.

Tom checked the activities room, but found only a
couple of residents lolling blankly, tongues protruding past
their lips. From the scraps and supplies left on the tables, it
appeared as though today's project had been Christmas card
ornaments. Great, Christmas in August.

A woman with tight white curls, crisp pants that
matched the ultra-white of the curls, and a pink-striped button down shirt, entered and whisked through the room, toss-

ing shards of paper into the trash, gathering safety scissors and glue sticks, and tidying unused cards. With her efficiency and good cheer, she might be mistaken for staff, but very few of the staff displayed either efficiency or good cheer. The woman, Jennie Day, was a willing resident of the nursing home, even though she was as spry as a spring lamb. Her husband, Samuel, had entered the institution after his diabetes became difficult to control, right around the same time Sara had come to the home. Jennie had moved in with Samuel so she could keep an eye on his care. When Samuel passed a year or so ago from gangrene and an unwillingness to undergo amputation, Jennie remained, having found a community that needed her brisk mothering. Samuel's business, a poultry processing plant a few miles southwest of Greenville, afforded her the financial means to stay.

"Say, Jennie," said Tom, interrupting her bustle, "You haven't seen Sara, have you?"

"Why, yes I have, Tom. She's in the sun room with that fine young man, Leroy. Having a good time with him, she is. I haven't seen her laugh so much in . . . well . . . forever. Why don't you scoot yourself in there and join them? Go on, now. Scoot. She'll be happy to see you." With that, Jennie returned to her self-appointed duties, darting around with more energy than the activity room knew what to do with.

Tom heard Sara before he saw her. She was around the back side of a hutch strategically placed inside the sun room door as a sort of privacy wall. Jennie was right. Sara was laughing, a soft, high hee-hee-hee, followed by a snort. Coaxing even a small smile out of Sara had become a near impossibility these past few months. Tom paused to listen. A low mellifluous voice responded to her delight. "Miss Sara, you are the prettiest gal in all of Greenville. And the sweetest, too."

A flush of heat poured from Tom's stomach into his limbs. He attributed it to the warmth of the room. From where he was standing, he could see the sun streaming at full capacity through the windows, where miscellaneous potted plants guzzled the opportunity to photosynthesize. He continued eavesdropping. Sara spoke next.

"No. You don't say," she replied, which sent another surge of heat through Tom and prickles up the back of his neck. Her Alzheimer's was so advanced that he thought she was incapable of such an intelligible response. When he spoke to her, he got little more than gibberish.

He considered leaving Sara in the company of the Tin Man. Obviously he was making a better connection with her than he ever could. *But, by God, she's my wife, not his.* With this thought, he maneuvered around the hutch and said, "You most certainly are the sweetest and prettiest gal in all of Greenville. No, make that in all the world."

The Tin Man sat next to Sara, holding her hand. Tom's appearance did nothing to dislodge the Tin Man's grasp.

"Look who's here, Sara." The Tin Man pointed to Tom with his free hand. "Look, right there, it's your husband, Tom."

Sara looked, but did not see. The question "Who?" floated through her mind, but got lost among the tangles of her brain before having even the whiff of a chance at reaching her mouth.

"It's me, Tom. Don't you know me?"

"Sure she knows you," said the Tin Man. "Give her a minute. Come, sit."

Tom pulled a chair up alongside Sara's wheelchair, opposite the Tin Man. He took Sara's other hand. She promptly yanked it away and spit out, "Don't touch me!" and leaned closer to the Tin Man. Tom recoiled. Anguish mapped crooked lines on his face. He didn't know what to say. Sara was oblivious to his hurt.

The Tin Man was not. He said, "She's having a bad day, is all. Not to worry." He turned back to Sara and patted her hand. She followed his voice and expressions with utmost concentration and a starry smile in her irises. "Let's try something, shall we, Miss Sara?" And then he did it. He launched into the bane of Tom's existence.

"Tom Twist
Made a list
Of all the girls
He hadn't kissed

"Becky, Susan, Molly, Karen
Rhoda, Lisa, Abby, Sharon

"Run, girls, run!
Here he comes!
Skitter, scatter
It doesn't matter

"Tom Twist
Just missed
All the girls
He hadn't kissed."

The utterance of the full rhyme set a torch aflame in
Tom's face, burning it like a full day's sun during his fish
squeezing days. Sweat trickled from under his arms down
his sides. He had worked his whole life to live down this
rotten ditty and now the Tin Man had the gall to use it
against him. Humiliate him in front of his wife. The automatic reflexes of childhood took over and Tom did the only
natural thing he could do in such a situation. He fled.

In the haste and blindness caused by his embarrassment,
he did not see the flicker of recognition in his wife's eyes.

A pint of Scotch whisky neat later and it was morning.
Tom was back at work, wiping down tables and polishing
the bar, even though Jake had made a thorough job of cleaning the night before.

It was his own damn fault. He'd put her in the nursing
home, a place she'd never wanted to be. Why hadn't he sold

the bar and stayed with her full time? Why hadn't he picked the nursing home across the river? It was a better facility, the staff more responsive to the residents' needs. He resisted the urge to argue himself out of the recriminations, conveniently negating the tortuous decisions he (and she) had made concerning her care.

She had become delusional, imagining things that were not there – people knocking with keys outside the upstairs windows of the house – their dead dog Jig nosing his water dish. Paranoia nipped the heels of delusion, with Sara thinking Tom was out to get her. She wouldn't eat anything he prepared for fear he had slipped in poison. He could have gotten use to the delusions, he supposed, and hired an in-home nurse to assist Sara with cooking and eating.

A nurse would have helped with the wandering, too, those times that Sara would take off into the streets and go. In her mind there was a valid reason for her travels, but when interrupted from her course and questioned, her explanations didn't make sense. There was the night Tom woke to find her gone from bed. Upon searching the house and seeing the front door flung wide, he ran out to discover her half-way down the next block. She was on her way to the doctor. At four a.m. In her nightgown. Going the wrong direction. He was now sure that better locks on the door would have prevented such forays.

Except for the time she had managed to make her way to the Green Street Bridge. That had been the turning point, really. She was trying to climb the railing when a passing motorist stopped and pulled her off. She couldn't understand the fuss people made about her wanting to go for a swim. He'd been this close to losing her to the river, and now he was losing her again, this time to the Tin Man. Chunk by giant chunk, she was going.

Tom ceased his obsessive counter polishing and sat on a bar stool, head in hands, sighing. No matter how much he told himself that it was the disease and not Sara doing this to him, it was hard not to take it personally. The essence of

Sara was still there. She liked the same music, tapping along to the sounds of the Big Band era, when he bothered to play it for her, and was attracted to the same sorts of decorative arts, thrilling over turquoise and silver jewelry, her favorite brown leather purse, and vases and knick-knacks made of blue glass. This was Sara stripped down, without any need for a husband. He choked at the thought and grew philosophical.

This is the pain of an individual shunned, that's what. How much of the definition of ourselves is wrapped up in other people's interactions with us? Who would I be, who would any of us be, if there wasn't a single soul left on earth?

Then, he became determined.

He would have to spend more time with Sara. He used to visit her every day in the home, so that she wouldn't feel abandoned. He'd been slipping this past year, whittling his time with her down to a measly once a week. No wonder she was chumming around with the Tin Man.

He arranged things with Jake and the endurance test began. Daily he visited, showing up at different times, hoping to catch Sara at her best and, most critically, without the Tin Man. It didn't happen often. Because the Tin Man had a calming effect on Sara, staff habitually placed them together – at mealtimes, activity hour, and sitting around waiting time, which was perpetual in the home. When Tom asked the staff not to seat them together, they refused to budge from the routine on the grounds that Sara was sullen and difficult to manage outside of his presence. "Don't you want your wife to be comfortable?" they had asked, making Tom out to be cross and insensitive.

He was too stubborn to simply ask the Tin Man to leave him alone with his wife. That would be admitting defeat, and he wasn't willing to concede her constancy to another man, no matter how little of his wife remained behind her bleary eyes.

The situation, the awkward stalemate of sharing his wife with the Tin Man, might have grown bearable over time if it hadn't been for that damn rhyme. Every time Tom showed up, the Tin Man introduced him to Sara with it. And he couldn't just recite the first couple of lines. He had to march through the entire thing. Line by mortifying line. Tom tolerated it as best he could, even though he wanted to pop the old guy. He cringed when Sara clapped and smiled upon the recitation. She knew how much he hated it and he blamed the Tin Man for her treason.

And then, one day, the stewing was over.

The atmosphere in the nursing home was joyful when Tom arrived. The staff was chatty and attentive to the residents for a change. The residents were chatty and energetic in return. Tom attributed the light mood to an unseasonably warm late fall day, a last hurrah before the gloom of winter descended.

He scoped out the public areas, and not seeing Sara, he asked a staff member, who pointed him in the direction of her room.

Déjà vu brushed him with the beeping of an unanswered call light along the corridor. It was coming from the Tin Man's room. He ducked in. The old man was shriveled into a misshapen ball on the bed, shivering. Tom looked him over, the men catching each other's eyes. The Tin Man communicated his inability to breathe with his stare and a phlegm-filled rasp.

The call light insisted that something be done.

Tom switched it off and left, closing the door softly behind him.

Story 10

Revelation

Look. See here. It's a funeral home. The reviewal room and chapel are one and the same. There are pews, so it feels like a church, except for the tissue boxes at the ends. Crying is not only expected, it's encouraged.

The walls are beige, nondescript, like in an apartment that receives tenants of all tastes. Only here it's about receiving tenants of all faiths, or no faith, and they call it nondenominational – a final church for the unchurched.

Funeral pyres are illegal, unless you want to enter an oven, where an enclosed flame will tickle you to the bone, dusting you right on down to the marrow, 'til you're no more than an eight-by-ten glossy and a baggy of asthma-inducing ash. In this state you could perhaps be added to coffee and no one would be the wiser, although ash might not have that non-dairy creamer sweetness.

The whole oven and death thing? That wasn't Leroy's way. He wanted to leave something more tangible behind, something exhumable and potentially archeological, mag-gots and beetles be damned. They would be welcome to the formaldehyde cocktail that had replaced his blood, if they could get through the cement vault and sealed casket.

There's Leroy now, being wheeled in by two crisp men in dark suits. You'll see him in a moment, once they lift the half-lid of his shiny silver box. The men are placing him at the front of the room, where he'll be easy to spot. The man of the hour.

You'll notice that his head is cricked at an odd angle, not for his eternal comfort, but for the viewing pleasure of the audience. It stands out against the pink satin lining, only it's not real satin by any means. That'd be too expensive to bury in the ground for all eternity. It merely has the appearance of satin and, if Leroy was alive, he'd be sweating all over its polyester sheen, what with the full military uniform he's wearing.

"He looks so natural." You'll hear that aplenty as the visitors drop in for the reviewal. You may even say it your-self. "So natural," as if it's the best compliment someone could pay the dead. The pancake makeup and blush sure beat the hell out of looking at a mottled purplish blue corpse, even though postmortem lividity is the height of true natu-ralness for Leroy at this juncture of his life. He never did care for keeping up appearances.

The crisp men in dark suits move about the room with practiced solemnity. It's getting too close to visiting hours to crack jokes, even though they have a million of them they're willing to share with you over a beer. But now's not the time or the place. A rude remark about the deceased overheard by unexpectedly early and sensitive ears would certainly squelch business. Instead, they busy themselves with accepting floral arrangements from the various local florists and quietly remark to each other about the unantici-pated volume the Tin Man is getting as they pull extra plant pedestals from storage and jostle vases and pots around to make room for them all. "Who'd a thunk a bum could be so popular?" is the sentiment they'll share with each other when it's all over.

Leroy waits patiently through the commotion, which promises to increase shortly.

Here they come, his family. Many of today's visitors will be surprised to find that the Tin Man has familial attach-ments, that he didn't sprout all of apiece from a dark void of random atoms or crawl out from under a cabbage leaf.

There's Stella, his niece, and her husband, Frank, his near-est living relatives, his parents and siblings having passed from this earth before he did. While Leroy has a number of nieces and nephews, Stella is the closest to him emotionally. The others thought him too kooky to get to know. Mind you, they won't say that here in his presence. They'll make excuses for distancing themselves. "We were too busy. We live too far away." What they are really saying is, "We were afraid the kookiness would rub off."

Stella and Frank are carrying items for an impromptu memorial display. Their children, Julie and Leroy, are assist-ing as mini pack mules. Stella juggles a small animal trap, a beaded bag of American Indian origin, and a vase of red, white, and blue carnations. Frank clutches a hinged bulletin board full of snapshots of Leroy. Stella put it together after finding an old cigar box full of photos in Leroy's footlocker. As they open it up, you'll see Leroy at different life stages.

There's one of him as a baby, sitting in his mother's lap, looking somber in his white, gauzy dress, which is a lumi-nous counterpoint to his dark face. There are several shots of him as a kid grinning for the camera while playing the violin at dances. Yes, he really could play, although you've probably only ever seen his violin case, *sans* violin, open on a street corner to collect change. He gave up the instrument long ago, when arthritis knotted his knuckles. His great-niece, Julie, is carrying that case and inside is the violin, now stringless. It's no Stradivarius, even though rumors to that effect have circulated about Greenville for years. That, and stories of Leroy's hidden wealth. But, there is no wealth. He was merely a guy trying to get by, and while he did pick out and pay for a burial plot in the Greenville Cemetery, Stella and Frank are subsidizing his funeral.

There are more snapshots to peruse. Here are some showing him with his Marine Corps buddies. This one is especially handsome. You can see the men in their dress uniforms. Leroy is fourth from the left. Leroy and the other guys had to pay for their own dress uniforms, fifty-four dollars a piece, because they weren't standard issue. While considered pricey at the time, the outfit has worn well and makes for inexpensive, yet formal, funeral attire. It's a bit loose now, but the funeral director artfully snugged it up so that it appears to fit properly.

Did you know that Leroy was a fish breeder after he got out of the military? Here are pictures of him and his crew on the Mud River netting and releasing fish. Those in the business call themselves fish squeezers because they literally squeeze the females to strip them of their eggs. The males are squeezed, too, their sperm getting mixed with the eggs. It was an enjoyable job for Leroy, right in line with his fur trapping ancestors. He got to be outdoors and meet a bunch of good guys, including one Mr. Tom Twist. You remember Tom, don't you? He owns a bar in downtown Greenville.

The picture board makes a great diversion. If you meet someone you don't know at the funeral and don't want to talk, you can turn to it and concentrate hard, pretending not to notice the stranger. If said stranger insists on launching into conversation, the photos provide subjects appropriate to small talk.

You can discuss how much or how little Leroy resembles his family, using the random pictures of his brothers and sisters or his parents' wedding portrait for comparison. You could even speculate on Leroy's love life, but you'll have to look sharp in order to spot the locket-sized portrait of his love, Pomeline Foil, tucked like a "Where's Waldo?" cartoon into the fabric of the photo collage. What might pass for gossip when Leroy was living is fair game now that both parties in the saga are gone.

Stella has finished arranging items by the picture board, with the exception of the things being carried by Young Leroy. The family calls him Young Leroy in order to distinguish him from the older Leroy because calling him Leroy Junior doesn't make sense in terms of the familial relationship. Inside Young Leroy's suit jacket pocket are his great-uncle's medals. He's a conscientious kid, so he keeps shoving his free hand into his pocket, checking to be sure the medals are still there. Crooked in his other arm is a framed portrait of Uncle Leroy in his dress uniform. Stella takes the portrait first and adds it to the memorial. Then she asks for the medals, which come out one-by-one. There's a World War II Victory Medal, a Legion of Merit Medal, and a Purple Heart, for when Uncle Leroy took shrapnel from a landmine in the rear end. Uncle Leroy used to say he didn't deserve the Purple Heart because he should've moved more carefully in landmine territory. "Damn stupid," he'd say when he talked about the incident. Embarrassment at where he was wounded was partially to blame for his feelings on the matter.

Young Leroy's legs are fidgety, wiggling and tapping as much as he thinks his father will allow. He would very much like you to notice his feet, specifically his shoes. After a good deal of searching, he finally got his brown Mary Janes, or as he publicly likes to call them, his Christopher Robins. His mom had to special order them over the internet from a company in England. He endured a bit of teasing at school for the first couple of weeks, until one of the popular kids decided the shoes were cool, particularly the fact that they had come from England, and suddenly there was a rash of brown Mary Janes appearing on the feet of kindergartners and first graders in Greenville.

The make-shift memorial is finished, minus one critical item - Leroy's pocket watch. It rests in Frank's interior jacket pocket, too precious for Frank to allow it to be put on display now that it is officially his. Leroy, aware of Frank's penchant for pragmatism and precise timekeeping, willed the watch to Frank, who had no qualms about accepting it, despite his feelings for the man in the coffin.

The funeral home attendants direct the Budsbanowski family to a back pew in order to confer with them about the details of the day. Young Leroy glances nervously at his great-uncle in the coffin and wonders if he can overhear their conversation.

The minister arrives, a young gal from the Greenville United Church of Christ. She gathers anecdotes from the family in order to weave them into a standard celebration of life service. While she was only marginally familiar with the living Leroy Jarbeau, she is adept at personalizing services such that today's visitors will think that she was a life-long friend of the decedent. The anecdotes are her salvation, although her kindness and genuine concern for all human beings, no matter how flawed, transmit the warmth of close-ness that the family will cling to in order to get through the ordeal. She makes it clear that smiling and laughing are as appropriate to the occasion as are tears.

The family is given a chance to say last words to Leroy, who has always been a good listener, but is displaying the skill in especially fine fashion today. Frank doesn't have much to say. He hadn't been fond of Leroy in life and he isn't going to make a hypocrite of himself by being fond of him in death. He is here for his wife and that's reason enough for him to follow the adage, "If you haven't got anything nice to say, don't say anything at all." Instead, he studies Leroy's makeup job and uniform for a respect-able amount of time and quietly says, "Goodbye, old man," before making a study of the botanical specimens on display. Their intrinsic beauty isn't the attractant, but the practicality of making room for all of them in the Blazer is. Frank likes solving practical problems.

Julie is next up to say her goodbyes. She and Young Leroy tussled a moment ago over who was not going to go first. Dead bodies have a high creep factor for their tender souls, Uncle Leroy being their very first real live dead body. His silence and woodenness do nothing to alleviate Julie's discomfort. What do you say to someone who doesn't ac-knowledge your presence? She follows the course of her fa-ther, examining her uncle closely, waiting for him to twitch. When he doesn't, she turns to her mother and says, "Is he still in there?" Stella replies, "No, sweetheart, Uncle Leroy's soul has left his body. He'll be going up to heaven soon, but he's probably hanging around watching all of us. Go ahead and tell him what you want. He'll hear you, I'm sure."

This news, the idea that Uncle Leroy's soul is still hanging around watching and listening, unsettles Julie more than the experience of a dead body. It is having the opposite effect on Young Leroy, who wishes Julie would get moving so he can talk. Julie murmurs a few general words about how much she liked coming to visit Uncle Leroy and winds up with a soft, "Love you," all the while imagining her uncle peering down at her and divining her true opinion of him. She has one foot in the camp of relatives who believed that Uncle Leroy was kooky. If you watch her closely during the rest of the reviewal and service, you'll notice that she keeps observing the air above her head, afraid to find her uncle hovering there.

Now that Young Leroy thinks the old Leroy can hear him, he marches up to the coffin and pays no mind to his uncle's stiffness and formality. He's got things to say and there'll be none of that whispering that everyone else engages in out of some misguided respect for the dead. If Uncle Leroy is only going to be around for a little while longer, no sense in speaking so quietly he can't hear.

"Hi, Uncle," he says. "Did you see my new shoes? I hope you like them. I wore them 'specially for you." He lifts his heel, preening unconsciously. "You sure look snazzy in that outfit. Mom let me try on your hat. I hope you don't mind. It didn't look right on me 'cause it's too big, but I bet it's perfect on you." Young Leroy turns to his mom and asks, "Why is his hat in his hands and not on his head?"

"Darling, it wouldn't sit right on his head with him lying down."

"Oh, okay. . . . . Anyway, Uncle, I want you to know I'm gonna miss you. And I'm gonna miss sharing pop with you and all the candy you gave me. My favorite was that one time you had jawbreakers. I know you couldn't eat them because of your teeth, but they looked so pretty and colorful in the candy dish, and I know you got them because of me and Julie. That was awfully nice of you.

"Mom's not gonna want me to say this because she thinks it's rude to talk about money, but I really, really like the silver dollars you gave me. They're so heavy, not like quarters. I wish all money felt that way 'cause it'd be hard to lose out of your pocket. Mom made me put them in the safe in our closet. I bet they're worth more than a dollar, aren't they? Otherwise, why would she make me put them in the safe?

"Anyway, Mom wants to talk to you." Young Leroy leans closer to his uncle so his mother won't hear this next part. "She's getting impatient, so I gotta tell you this quick. I'm glad you wore two different shoes, even if people thought you were strange for doing so. It makes me feel not so weird about my shoes. I love you, Uncle. I'll miss you. Have fun in heaven. Here's Mom now."

Stella takes her time bidding farewell to Leroy and finishes by kissing him on the cheek, which leaves an imprint on Julie's mind that will bother her like a menacing shadow seen from the corner of an eye. Young Leroy remains unfazed by the display of necrotic affection. He wishes he had thought to give Uncle Leroy a kiss, too.

People are starting to drift in now. Frank and Stella take their places by the entry, greeting friends and family and the merely curious, who believe they personally know the Tin Man because he was such a regular fixture on the streets of Greenville. Like the sudden removal of lamp posts or stop signs or an unusual tree in the park, the death of the Tin Man has caused the merely curious to realize that they can, indeed, miss that which is normally overlooked.

Perhaps this is how you feel as you sift through the crowd looking for recognizable faces. While you've gotten pretty familiar with Greenville during your stay, there are plenty here who do not register with the memories you have on file. In fact, individuals you meet today may not properly register later should you run across them, the volume of new faces being too much for your overworked dendrites to latch onto. Instead, you focus on those you do know and make polite, but inconsequential conversation with those you don't, opting for the role of observer whenever humanly possible.

Greenville's mayor, Tallulah "Loofah" Lufkins, manages to stop by, as well as several city council members. Somehow they've arranged to come in shifts so as not to give the appearance of conducting an unofficial meeting. Through a bit of artful eavesdropping, purely defensible behavior when done at a public funeral, you manage to gather that Leroy Jarbeau attended city council meetings at least twice a month for years, going back as far as anyone can remember. Oftentimes, other than a reporter from the *Greenville Gazette*, he was the only citizen in attendance – the sole persistent voice speaking on behalf of Every Man.

This is not the only thing you learn about the Tin Man. The owner of Spolvero Meats, Dan Spolvero, reveals to his sister, Nancy, and her husband, Rudy, that the Tin Man used to come into the store regularly, mostly to chat. If he had enough cash from his Social Security check or from recycling aluminum cans, he'd buy a few sausages or a rib-eye steak. For Christmas, he'd get a jar of pickled herring. Dan admits that he felt sorry for the old guy, which led him to slip a little extra into the butcher paper packages he wrapped up for the Tin Man. The happy result of this small action made Dan feel generous, like he was doing his part in alleviating hunger, and added a few much-needed calories to the Tin Man's diet.

You ask about Rudy and Nancy's daughters and discover that they are at home with a sitter. Nancy explains that the girls are too young to attend a funeral for someone they did not know. Dan, Nancy and Rudy excuse themselves in order to view the body and you continue to mingle at the edges of small conversational clusters.

Maureen Lestico is telling Mayor Lufkins that Leroy's house belongs on the National Register of Historic Places while she balances a toddler on her hip. Those museum types, they're always trying to save buildings. She does make a good point when she says that the houses of ordinary people are rarely deemed worthy enough to save. The houses of poor people, like the Tin Man, are considered even less worthy, but by saving only the impressive homes, society's picture of history gets skewed. This is part of Maureen's argument and you know that it's going to take far more convincing to get the city council to buy into her plan of making the house an informal tourist attraction. As you listen to her explain how this can happen in a practical, low-cost manner, you wonder about the child she holds. Is this the one she fished out of the river?

Behind you, sitting at the end of a pew, a woman startles you by responding to your question. "No, that's not the same child." You didn't think that you had uttered your question aloud.

"Sorry," the woman says, "I didn't mean to pry, but I'm in scanning mode and happened to catch your thought. People are more open to the other side during funerals, less guarded in general, because of all the emotion." Before you can muster a reply, she says, "Maureen is a foster mom now. Dolly is her first foster child."

Ah, yes, how could you forget? This is the librarian/medium with the exotic name – Araminta. It's time for a test. You think: *What happened to the river baby? What was its name again?* And you wait for an answer.

"Maureen called the baby Reed, but that wasn't his given name. The mother doesn't want his real name released for privacy reasons. She has him back and lets Maureen visit when she likes. Aunty Momo, she is. It was a desperate situation that got out of hand, but seems to have straightened itself out well enough." She looks at you with a gaze that could drill for oil and says, "You know, playing a game of 'Test the Medium' is old hat. Why don't you ask me directly?"

It's your turn to apologize and you do so, following up with another question. This time you ask aloud. "Is he still here?" You gesture toward the casket.

"Oh, sure. Why wouldn't he be? You don't have to be a medium to feel his presence in the room. All of us are carrying some of Leroy's energy with us. He'll stick around as long as a bunch of us are gathered and concentrating on him. See that girl over there?" She points to Leroy's great-niece, Julie, and says, "See how she keeps glancing at the ceiling? She thinks he's up there, but he's really surrounding us. The soul does not stay the same size as the body, but expands and diffuses after death."

Suddenly, Araminta sits up and eyes the entry. You follow her attention. "I've been expecting him," she says, and stands to go join a young man who is giving his condolences to Frank and Stella. It's Monroe Dobbs, the sound healer.

There was quite the hubbub in Greenville when he decided to stop his healing sessions and move in with his sister. You watched the story closely in the *Greenville Gazette*. His church and his manager, Sheldon Rhodes, tried to sue him for breach of contract. As it turned out, there were plenty of contracts, but not one specifically with Monroe, even though one was produced. As the case progressed, it was revealed that Emanuel Dobbs, Monroe's father, in cahoots with the manager, had drawn up a contract after the fact in order to bolster their case and had forged Monroe's signature to make it look legitimate. The contract wasn't the real issue. Unpaid employment taxes and child labor laws were. The judge ruled that the church, manager, and Emanuel had been taking advantage of a minor, and found all parties guilty of tax evasion. The requisite penalties and interest were tacked onto the back taxes. Emanuel and Sheldon were fined for the forgery and the church was directed to start a trust fund for Monroe using proceeds earned from the healing sessions. Further, the judge appointed Monroe's sister Jenna as his guardian.

You wonder at the sort of conversation that might take place between a medium and a sound healer. As your imagination gets going, it's short-circuited by the sight of a man doing an impression of a tattered rag. He's faded, holey, and frayed around the edges. The chapel isn't big enough for him to hide in, but he's doing his best to tuck himself into corners where no corners exist. Unkempt though he is, with his long, kinky graying hair, full beard and moustache, he reminds you of the western world's stereotypical image of an old Biblical character. He's already got the sandals; all he needs is a robe.

Sandals. Current weather conditions, six inches of the season's first snow accessorized by a plunging thermometer, preclude the use of sandals for anyone in their right mind. Ah, but you've heard that this guy isn't in his right mind. The sandals have tipped you off. This is the man that everyone calls Johnny Jesus Boots. Until this moment, you have not encountered him in the flesh, but you've heard plenty about him. He's known as a street crazy, but boards at a group home. He is let out often enough to cause perpetual anxiety in those wearing masks of comfortable sanity. He does this by inflicting them with his peculiar brand of religiosity, but he doesn't do it directly, like an evangelical preacher would. He does it by means of an interior monologue that rambles forth, vocalized in such a fashion that it draws you in, enchanted.

Johnny Jesus Boots has found himself a chair at the back of the chapel, where he is rocking and maundering. As you move closer to him, you hear him proselytizing.

"Gotta accept Christ, gotta accept Christ. Too much sin, repent, repent. Forgive me Father, for I have sinned."

You are not certain that he's aware of the event going on around him, of the dead body at the front of the room, until you catch his next words.

"Going to our Savior. Tin Man. Going to our Savior. Holy, holy, holy Lord. Uh oh. Tin Man. Forgive him Father, for he has sinned. It's not the sinner; it's the sin. Sinner. Sinner." He sees that you are staring at him and finishes with, "Sinner."

You back away. Your own mask of comfortable sanity

has slipped and you search the room for a means to reattach it. You find it in the form of Lenore St. Cyr and Sully Clark, who are moving gracefully amongst the crowd, talking with acquaintances, admiring the flowers, and telling Leroy Jarbeau that he looks so natural. They interact with one another in such consonance that some might assume they have long been married. This is not the case. They are simply friends who are leading each other back to the path of fruitful living. Sully is drinking less and Lenore is taking courses that will allow her to finish her teaching degree – small maneuvers that grow a yard of hope and a foot of happiness. Their joy is enough for you to shake the apprehension caused by Johnny Jesus Boots.

A commotion that you cannot ignore erupts near the coffin. One of the crisp men in dark suits is directing some heated words toward a group of children. You can't make out the words, but you can tell they are heated from the creases in the crisp man's face. You and much of the rest of the crowd push forward to ascertain the reason for his annoyance. After bobbing and tiptoeing to get a better view through the heads that separate you from the action, you recognize the children. It's Chris Dickle and her merry band of buddies. They appear to have a large, black garbage bag filled practically to bursting. Chris is waving a smashed pop can in one hand, trying to convince the crisp man that she has every right to leave her group's collection of cans for the Tin Man. The room goes silent, everyone suddenly struck mute by the unfolding drama.

"You'll do no such thing," says the crisp man. "Now turn around and take that filthy bag out of here before I throw you all out. It's disgraceful."

Chris replies with, "It's not disgraceful and we're not leaving. It's the Tin Man's funeral, not yours, and the Tin Man would appreciate the gesture."

"It may be the Tin Man's funeral, but I work here and what I say goes. Where are your parents?"

"Our parents have nothing to do with this."

"They will when I get through with you."

"Excuse me?" Stella roars from the back of the chapel. With her hands on her hips, she cuts through the crowd, elbows promising to jab whoever gets in her way. "Are you threatening these children?"

"No, ma'am, I just . . . ."

"You just nothing. I'm paying for this funeral and these kids have my permission to leave their bag of cans for Leroy. Do you understand?"

"Yes, ma'am." The crisp man sulks off.

"Go ahead now, children, find a good place to put your bag," says Stella. "Make sure everyone can see it."

Chris asks, "Can I put some on the coffin, please? If it's not too many?"

"Sure, darling. Knock yourself out. Leroy would've gotten a kick out of it."

Few eyes remain dry in the chapel as Chris reverently places four crushed pop cans in a line on top of the Tin Man's coffin. Even Tom Twist, that tough old fish squeezer, grabs a tissue from the box sitting next to him on the front pew.

Are you surprised to see him at the funeral? You shouldn't be. If the Tin Man could speak, have a few final words with you, he'd say, "Tom's a good man. He did the right thing."